Balthasar Münter, Jorgen Hee

A Faithful Narrative of the Conversion and Death of Count Struensee

To which is added The history of Count Enevold Brandt - The whole translated from the original German

Balthasar Münter, Jorgen Hee

A Faithful Narrative of the Conversion and Death of Count Struensee
To which is added The history of Count Enevold Brandt - The whole translated from the original German

ISBN/EAN: 9783337402433

Printed in Europe, USA, Canada, Australia, Japan

Cover: Foto ©Andreas Hilbeck / pixelio.de

More available books at **www.hansebooks.com**

A

FAITHFUL NARRATIVE

OF THE

CONVERSION AND DEATH

OF

COUNT STRUENSEE,

Late PRIME MINISTER of DENMARK;

Together with

LETTERS of his PARENTS to Him, and also a LETTER of his own; wherein he relates how he came to alter his SENTIMENTS of RELIGION.

Publiſhed by D. MUNTER,

An EMINENT DIVINE, who was ordered by the KING to prepare him for Death.

TO WHICH IS ADDED,

THE HISTORY

OF

COUNT ENEVOLD BRANDT,

From the Time of his Impriſonment to his Death.

Together with two ANONYMOUS LETTERS, found in his Pocket-Book, wherein he was forewarned of what happened to him Four Months after; and likewiſe an EXACT COPY of his SENTENCE.

The Whole tranſlated from

THE ORIGINAL GERMAN.

Embelliſhed with the Heads and Coats of Arms of both the unhappy COUNTS.

LONDON:

Printed for U. LINDE, Stationer, in Bridges-Street, Covent-Garden. MDCCLXXIII.

ADVERTISEMENT

OF THE

TRANSLATOR.

MOST accounts which are given of conversions of hardened sinners, are drawn up with more enthusiasm than reason, and are too frequently embellished with declamations, tales, dreams, and other insignificant trifles; so that Christians, who are better acquainted with the true spirit of our divine religion, must be offended by them; and others, who are no friends of religion, will certainly turn them into ridicule, and harden themselves in their unbelief and immorality. The Translator took the original of this book

A 2

into

into his hand with prepossessions of this kind; but he found himself agreeably deceived, and thought it, after an attentive reading, capable of promoting the cause of true religion and real virtue, for both which he is not ashamed to profess himself a warm advocate. With this view he undertook the translation of it, fearing that in this, as well as in all other nations, there are but too many whose principles of religion and morality are similar to those of Struensee, and who indulge themselves, according to their stations and opportunities, full as much as he did, in every passion and vice which proved his ruin.

There is one thing which must recommend this account to the particular attention of the reader; and that is, its authenticity: for there is not the least doubt in this respect, which the Translator could not engage to satisfy, if it was required; but he trusts, that a candid perusal of the work itself will afford sufficient evidence of its being genuine. D. Munter, who is the undoubted Author of the account concerning Struensee, is an eminent Divine,

and

and Rector of one of the principal German churches at Copenhagen; and the character he bears is sufficient to establish its veracity. The same must be said of the History of Count Brandt, which was written by D. Hee. These clergymen were specially appointed by the King of Denmark, to attend the two respective state prisoners; and therefore the English reader is desired to remove all unfavourable impressions, which are generally annexed to publications of gaol ordinaries.

As to the translation, the Translator owns, that it would be the highest presumption in him to pretend to any elegance of style; he being a Foreigner, who, but a few years ago, was entirely unacquainted with the English language. He hopes, therefore, the candid English reader, who is master of his native tongue, will overlook the faults he may here happen to meet with.—He further declares, that though he is sure he has not wilfully mistaken the original, which he may be supposed to be in some measure

A 3

a master

a master of, from his education and profession, yet he has, according to the rule of Horace, not translated word for word; and many places where the good Doctors appeared to him a little declamatory, and too prolix in explaining speculative doctrines, he has partly left out, and partly abridged; and he is now, after the whole is finished, so far from thinking that he has done wrong in this respect, that he rather wishes he had left out a great deal more. Nevertheless, every thing of importance is translated, and those passages which are Struensee's own words are, together with his letter to D. Munter *and all other letters through the whole book, translated* verbatim; *and the English reader, who is wholly unacquainted with the language of the original, and therefore enabled to peruse the translation only, may rely upon his reading a faithful one.*

D. MUNTER's PREFACE.

MANY reafons have induced me to relate the falutary reformation of Count Struenfee. He has made much noife in the world. Every thing that is written about him is read with eagernefs. Perhaps this account may be perufed with utility, and even excite the attention of thofe who are of the fame way of thinking as Struenfee formerly was, to reflect ferioufly on religion and morality. He himfelf wifhed that thofe, who through him were feduced to a contempt of religion and morality, or were only mifled in their notions of religion and virtue, might be made acquainted of his return to truth and better fentiments, and of the manner in which he was reformed. He

hoped

hoped that by this means, thofe bad impreffions might be effaced, which he had made upon their minds.——Laftly, his converfion will reconcile him again to the virtuous, whom his principles and his example might have offended.

That I may the better convince my readers, of the truth of what I relate, I have chofen to give an account of every fingle interview I had with him. I never went to him unprepared. I meditated on every fubject firft, and then wrote it down. As foon as I came home, I entered in my journal what had happened and what he faid, and wherever I have introduced him fpeaking, it is as near as poffible in his own words.

Some things which I relate may be looked upon as trifling, but fenfible readers will oftentimes find the character of a perfon placed in a ftronger light by thefe trifles, and then they ceafe to be fuch, and do not deferve this name.

The

The books I gave from time to time to the Count, and which he perufed with attention, filled up many vacancies in my inftruction. They prepared him for that which followed, and enlightened his underftanding more in one month, than by mere converfation could have been done in twelve.

How the account given by Struenfee himfelf in his own writing arofe, I have related in the courfe of the narrative itfelf. But is it true that he wrote it himfelf? His hand-writing is well enough known in Denmark, the paper he wrote upon was given him by his judges, every fheet was numbered and figned by them, and could reach no other perfons hands but his.—But have I dictated to him the contents? I declare that it fully can be proved, that he, during my abfence, filled up thofe fheets, which were marked, and were given him one by one, and were delivered up again in the fame manner. But is what he has drawn up, and which I publifh here, a true account,

count, is it agreeable to the original? Whoever entertains doubts of this kind, may infpect the original itfelf, which is in my poffeffion, or may take it along with him for a time, fufficient to compare it with the copy. I thought it neceffary to mention all thefe particulars, becaufe I know, how little the narrative of a clergyman, concerning the converfion of a deift, is credited by thofe, whofe party he has left. They always are ready to fay: It is all impofition. However, they certainly will not be able to prove it in this inftance. If they fhould fay, that Struenfee turned chriftian through fear, or that he was out of his mind, or that I ftunned him with my declamations; I muft leave it to them to judge as they think proper.

My intention in publifhing what Struenfee with his own hand has drawn up, is to make it appear, that he himfelf had attentively confidered his former fyftem as well as chriftianity, and that, after fuch a mature confideration, he was induced to

quit

quit the former, and to embrace the latter.

An accuracy in ideas and expreſſions, no body will expect in the writings of a man, who ſtudied religion but a few months, who through the whole courſe of his former life thought very little of it, and who never wrote a word about it. If it ſhould be found entirely wanting in ſome places, I hope every chriſtian (and every chriſtian will judge according to charity) will not charge him with hereſy, which was (even the name of it) unknown to him. The chief point, that he died truſting in the mercy of God through Chriſt Jeſus, with ſentiments as well re-formed as could be done without a miracle, I hope no body will diſpute. But I ſcarce dare to judge of the merit of this conver-ſion, ſince it concerns me too much, and I wiſh too ardently that every one may believe it to be a ſincere one; even this ſhews me the danger I am in, of deceiving myſelf in my opinion. Therefore, having

here

(xii)

here faithfully given the narrative of this converfion, I leave it to fenfible and judicious chriftians to determine concerning the probability of it.

I do not know whether I have occafion to declare, that by the account which I give here, my intention is neither to render the Count's memory odious, nor to apologize for him. Thofe who on account of his crimes, have juft reafon to be prejudiced againft him, will now think it their duty to forgive him, and to pity his former infatuation. Thofe who find his behaviour in the latter part of his life decent and becoming a chriftian, will not forget what he was before, and how inevitably he drew his melancholy fate upon himfelf.

Copenhagen, June the 22d, 1772,

ERRATUM.
P. 80. l. 14. for *now found*, read *formerly thought.*

THE

THE HISTORY

OF THE

CONVERSION

OF

COUNT STRUENSEÉ.

COUNT Struenſee had, neither before nor during the time of his greateſt proſperity, ſhewn himſelf a religious or a moral man, at leaſt no one could think him to be ſuch; his own example, ſome of his public regulations, and his aboliſhing ſuch laws as were made to reſtrain vice and immorality, ſeemed clearly to prove, that the general opinion concerning his ſentiments of religion was not altogether ill founded. Whoever had the moſt favourable opinion of him, thought him an inconſiderate man, who had given himſelf up entirely to pleaſure and ambition, and who perhaps might recover from his errors. But all ſenſible people agreed in this, that during his adminiſtration religion had every thing to fear, and that the

morals

morals of the people, at leaſt in the metropolis, were in danger of becoming wild and ungovernable.

Theſe reflections occaſioned many honeſt and good people, who are incapable of rejoicing at the misfortunes of others, to look upon the 17th of January, the day when Struenſee fell, as one of the happieſt days in their life: they ſaw the rights of virtue and piety ſecured from that danger which ſeemed to threaten them; they wiſhed that the man, from whom no more was to be feared, and whoſe unhappy fate might eaſily be foretold, would acknowledge his errors and his crimes, and that God afterwards would grant him mercy.

When by the committee that was appointed to enquire into his affairs, ſo much was diſcovered that it was ſure his life would fall a ſacrifice to public juſtice, I received the King's orders to viſit him in his priſon, and to mind the welfare of his ſoul. I did not know the man, nor did he know me; and as to our principles and ſentiments, they were to all appearance very different. I had even to expect that my profeſſion and the intent I viſited him with would make him diſtruſt me; on the other hand, I had little reaſon to put great confidence in him. However, I entertained ſome hopes, that in his preſent ſituation he might find even a con-

verſation

verfation with a clergyman not quite infupport-
able; and the compaffion I had for him would
never permit me to prepoffefs him againft me
by fevere and ill-timed expoftulations. Befides,
I was told by fome of his former acquaintance,
that he was open, and in fome refpects fincere;
I thought it therefore not impoffible to efta-
blifh a friendfhip between us that might promote my intention concerning him. With thefe
hopes I began to vifit him, and I praife God for
the bleffing he has granted to my labours.

The firft Conference. March the firft, 1772.

I Could at prefent have no other view but
only to lay fome foundation for our mutual
confidence, and to make him look upon the
intention of my vifits as important, and, when
an opportunity fhould offer, to know his fentiments about religion.

When he was told I was there, and wifhed to
fpeak to him, he enquired whether I came by
command? being anfwered in the affirmative,
he complied. He received me with a four and
gloomy countenance, in the attitude of a man
who was prepared to receive many fevere reproaches, with a filence that fhewed contempt.
We were alone, and I was greatly moved, be-
holding the mifery of a man who, but a few

 weeks

weeks ago, was the firſt and the moſt powerful of all the King's ſubjects. I could neither hide my feelings, nor would I. Good Count, ſaid I, you ſee I come with a heart that is ſenſibly affected for you: I know and feel my obligations towards an unhappy man, whom God, I am ſure, never intended to be born for ſuch a misfortune. I ſincerely wiſh to make my viſits, which I am ordered to pay you, agreeable and uſeful.—Here he quitted his affected attitude, his countenance grew more ſerene, he gave me his hand, and thanked me for the ſhare I took in his fate. Our converſation, continued I, will be now and then diſagreeable both to you and me; but I profeſs moſt ſolemnly, that I ſhall tell you even theſe melancholy truths, which I have to communicate to you, without ſeverity, and even with pain to myſelf. I know I have no right to give you any unneceſſary uneaſineſs, and you may depend upon my ſincerity. Should it happen that accidentally in our converſation a word ſhould ſlip from me which perhaps may appear offenſive, I declare beforehand that it never was ſaid with ſuch a deſign, and I beg that in ſuch inſtances you will overlook my precipitation. With an air and a look that appeared to me not very favourable, he replied, " Oh! you may ſay what you pleaſe."

I ſhall

I fhall certainly, good Count, fay nothing but what my great defire to contribute towards your future happinefs, as much as lies in my power, fhall oblige me to. I wifh to raife your attention to a ferious confideration of your moral ftate, and how you ftand in regard to God. You do not know how your fate in this world may be decided, and chriftianity, which I teach and believe, makes it my duty earneftly to wifh for your everlafting happinefs. Confider my vifits and my converfation only in this view, and I hope you will not difapprove of them. I had feveral reafons to decline the King's order which brings me to you: but the hope of com-forting you in your misfortunes, and of advifing you to avoid greater ones, was too important for me. Do not charge me with views of a meaner fort. I come not for my own fake, but only with an intent of being ufeful to you. He then confeffed twice that he was fully con-vinced, I did it for his own advantage.

If you are convinced of this, continued I with an emotion of heart, grant me then that confi-dence, which you cannot refufe a man, who is anxious for your welfare. I fhall return it with the moft thankful friendfhip, although you in the beginning fhould take me for a weak and prejudiced man. I fhall not be tired in this

friend-

friendſhip, but endeavour to make it uſeful to you, ſince I am your only friend upon earth, and ſince you certainly will call upon your only friend for comfort. Here he ſtared at me, as I think, with tears in his eyes, and preſſed me by the hand.

I found him moved, and endeavoured to make uſe of this advantageous moment. If you wiſh to receive that comfort, ſaid I, which, in my opinion, I can promiſe you as the only true one, do not cheriſh that unhappy thought of dying like a philoſophical hero; for I doubt whether you will be able to keep it up to the end. I am afraid your courage will leave you at laſt, though perhaps you may force yourſelf to ſhew it outwardly. Firmneſs and tranquillity of mind, on the near approach of · death, is certainly the effect only of a good conſcience. " In all my adverſities," anſwered he, " I have ſhewn firmneſs of mind, and agreeably to this character, I hope I ſhall die not like an hypocrite." Hypocriſy, ſaid I, in ſuch moments, would be ſtill worſe than an affected firmneſs, though even this would be a kind of hypocriſy. In caſe of death, do not truſt to your former reſolution, and do not compare your former adverſities, which were perhaps nothing but ſickneſs and diſtreſs, with that fate which is now

ready

ready to fall upon you.—But perhaps you entertain fome hopes of faving your life?—"No!" faid he, "I flatter myfelf with no hopes at all."—But you do not fee death near you, faid I; you do not know the time when you fhall leave this world? Perhaps it is at fome months diftance. But, (here I took him by the hand) my dear Count, fuppofe I was ordered to tell you that you was to die to-day cr to-morrow; would not your courage fail? "I do not know," faid he. But, continued I, if your courage fhould leave you, and it was then too late to look out for comfort and hope, how do you think your heart would ftand affected? He anfwered nothing. You fee by this that the intent of our converfation is of great importance to you, and deferves all your attention. I aim at nothing lefs, than to prepare you for eternity, that it may be a happy one. But I muft expect that we are not both of the fame opinion, in regard to the ftate of man after death. Yet, though you might have perfuaded yourfelf that there is no life to come, and confequently neither rewards nor punifhments, I cannot help thinking that there never was a time, when you were fully convinced of it. Your inward feelings have frequently contradicted you. The thought of eternity frightened you, though unfortunately

you

you had art enough to ftifle it in its birth.—
However, it will be always out of your power
to prove that there is no eternity.

He heard me with attention, but he would
not own that he ever had any inward impreffions
of immortality, or had been afraid of it. Perhaps he might have been, but he did not recollect it. He owned the thought, that he fhould
foon entirely ceafe to be, was difagreeable to
him ; it frightened him, he wifhed to live, even
if it were with lefs happinefs than he now enjoyed
in his prifon. But he added, he did not find the
thought of total annihilation fo terrible as he had
found it was to many, who entertained the fame
fentiments with him,

I continued, You cannot deny the poffibility
of a future life, for there is at leaft as much
probability for it as there is againft it. I believe
I could evince from mere reafon, that eternity
is highly probable, which in fuch cafes amounts
almoft to certainty. But fuppofe it was only
probable, which you muft agree to, it is even
then a matter of great importance to you, for
you to know what may perhaps happen to
you hereafter. In cafe you had to fear an unhappy life, you fhould prepare yourfelf againft it,
or make it at leaft tolerable.—He agreed to this,
but added, " You will hardly make me believe
that

that there is a future life, and though you perhaps may convince my underſtanding by reaſons which I cannot overthrow, my heart however will not yield to the conviction. My opinion, which is oppoſite to your's, is ſo ſtrongly woven into my ſentiments; I have ſo many arguments in favour of it; I have made ſo many obſervations from anatomy and phyſic, which confirm it, that I think it will be impoſſible for me to renounce my principles. This however I promiſe, that I will not wilfully oppoſe your endeavours to enlighten me, but rather wiſh, as far as it lies in my power, to concur with you. I will not diſſemble, but honeſtly tell you of what I am convinced, and of what I am not. I will deal with you openly; this is my character, and my friends can bear witneſs to it." In our enquiries, I deſired him to guard againſt his careleſs way of thinking, to which, in my opinion, he had been hitherto addicted, and which had thrown him into this depth of miſery. He anſwered :

" I do not deny my having lived inconſiderately in the world, and I feel now the conſequences of it."

I truſt in your promiſe, added I, that you will deal with me honeſtly. If you did not, you would impoſe upon me, though perhaps but for

a few

a few days. But you certainly cannot deceive the Supreme Being and your own confcience. It would give me the higheft pleafure if my intentions fhould fucceed. But befides the affiftance of God, you muft do all the reft your-felf. I can only guide you, and it is your own intereft to mind your welfare, and you are obliged to employ all the time which is left you upon this bufinefs.

I afterwards defired him to acquaint me with his fyftem of religion, that I might be able to judge, where our opinions differed. I am in-clined to think you are not a chriftian, and you may eafily guefs how much I wifh you to be one. It is not my intention to force chriftianity upon you; but I hope to reprefent it to you as fo important and amiable, that you yourfelf will think you ftand greatly in need of it. He anfwered:

" It was true, he was very far from being a chriftian, though he acknowledged and adored a Supreme Being, and believed that the world and mankind had their origin from God.—He could never perfuade himfelf, that man confifted of two fubftances. He looked upon himfelf and all other men as mere machines; he had borrowed this fyftem, not from de la Mettrie, whofe book he had never read, but had formed

it

it by his own meditation. It was God that firſt animated this human machine; but as ſoon as its motion ceaſed, that is, when man died, there was no more for him either to hope or to fear. He did not deny that man was endowed with ſome power of liberty, but his free actions were determined only by his ſenſations. Therefore, man's actions could be accounted moral, only as far as they related to ſociety. Every thing that man could do, was in itſelf indifferent. God did not concern himſelf about our actions, and if their conſequences were in man's own power, and he could prevent their being hurtful to ſociety, nobody had a right to reproach him about them. He added, he muſt own, that he was very ſorry for ſome of his actions, and in particular, that he had drawn others with him into misfortunes; but he feared no bad conſequences or puniſhments after this life. He could not ſee, why ſuch puniſhments were neceſſary to ſatiſfy the juſtice of God, even though he allowed that God minded our actions. Man was puniſhed already enough in this world for his tranſgreſſions. He himſelf was certainly not happy during the time of his greateſt proſperity. He had, at leaſt during the laſt months of it, to ſtruggle with many diſagreeable paſſions.—One of his principal ob-

jections

jections againſt chriſtianity was, that it was not univerſal. If it were really a divine revelation, it abſolutely ſhould have been given to all mankind."

I ſaid at this time but little to anſwer all this, but recommended to him an excellent book, which, as I hoped, would contribute towards clearing up his ideas about religion. He aſked, with a kind of diffidence, " What book ?" Jeruſalem's Conſiderations on the principal Truths of Religion, ſaid I ; a book which you will read with pleaſure, if it even was only for the elegance of its ſtile. He deſired me to bring it to him.

I had obſerved, that he was really very uneaſy about ſome of his actions, and I thought proper to encreaſe his uneaſineſs. I ſuppoſe my readers know how much he was to be blamed for his conduct towards count Bernſtorf *. I acquainted him, therefore, upon taking my leave of him, with his death. He called out with an emotion of heart : " What, is he dead ?" and ſeemed to ſhudder. Yes, ſaid I, he is. His wiſdom, religion, and piety, have preſerved him the

* Count Bernſtorf was miniſter of ſtate in Denmark ſince the year 1750. Struenſee got this great and beloved miniſter diſmiſſed, by a letter of the king's, dated September the 15th, 1770, with a penſion of 6000 crowns ; he retired to Hamburgh, where he died the 18th of February, 1772.

character

character of a great man to the laſt; and it is generally believed, that the grief of his laſt years had haſtened his death. When I ſpoke this, I looked at him with an air which he ſeemed to underſtand, for he bluſhed.

The ſecond Conference. March the third.

THE firſt thing I had to do now, with Count Struenſee, was to convince him of the falſity of his ſyſtem, that man was a mere machine. For hence he concluded, that there was no future life. Beſides, as he looked upon eternity as a mere fable, he could not regard religion and morality.

I reminded him of his promiſe, not to oppoſe truth wilfully, but rather to meet it half way. You think your opinion, ſaid I, of man's being a mere machine, to be true, and you conclude from thence more, than there is in reality foundation for. However, I preſume, you think this opinion of yours is no more than a philoſophical hypotheſis, and in this view let us conſider it to day. It is not very neceſſary to enter into a particular conſideration of it, for it cannot be proved from thence, that there is no futurity. However, let us conſider it, that you may not think I intend to ſurprize you.—When I had

2   exhauſted

exhausted all my arguments and reasonings, I found they had but little effect upon his understanding. At last he owned, that the hypothesis, of the existence of a soul, was better founded than his. But he said, he had good reasons to maintain his former sentiments ; for the knowledge of man, was in general very uncertain. He might, perhaps, hitherto have imposed upon himself : but he was liable, as often as he adopted a new opinion, to be deceived. Besides, his mind was, in his present situation, neither composed nor serene enough to examine his present principles. He should have done this sooner ; it was now too late. Several things being replied, the whole concluded with a serious and tender exhortation, not to let the few last weeks of his life slip away useless for eternity, but to do his best, to enter into it with good hopes. He then looked very earnestly at me, and casting down his eyes, replied :

" You must have a great deal of goodness, humanity, and faithfulness of a minister, since you are so anxious about my welfare, and are not displeased at my not agreeing with you exactly in opinion."

I assure you, continued I, I shall not, until the very last day of your life, desist from exhorting and intreating you, and I hope God will

bless

blefs my endeavours. But, good Count, I am afraid of your unhappy difpofition, which has contributed fo much to your misfortune; your ambition, and your defire to be always in the right, prevents your doing juftice to truth. How is it poffible, that you can be ftill fond of an inclination, which has thrown you into fuch a mifery?

" Oh! faid he, this inclination is gone, I am now very little in my own eyes; and how could I be ambitious in this place!" This paf-fion, anfwered I, rages certainly ftill in your foul. The occafions of fhewing itfelf as for-merly are only wanting. But though it may oppofe the truth, if you indulge it, yet take heed, left defpifed truth fhould revenge itfelf.

Since it was now greatly my intereft, to foften his heart for humane and tender feelings, for by this I hoped to make way for religion; I begged him to confider, how infinitely he had afflicted his parents, and how much it, therefore, was his duty, to ufe all his endeavours to procure them that only comfort which was left them, not to be anxious about his future ftate. He anfwered, " My father is an honeft man, he acts according to his own fentiments; but I believe he has treated me too feverely." You may think fo, faid I, but I fancy you are mif-taken.

taken. Without doubt you have been extravagant from your very youth, which your honeſt father diſapproved. This you called ſeverity. " This is true, but"—But, ſaid I, you knew he was father, and you ſon. Were you ignorant that you owed obedience to your father, who was beſides an honeſt man ? " I was dutiful to a certain age." But, ſaid I, were you after certain years leſs ſon, and he leſs father? Confucius, whoſe moral ſyſtem, as I remember to have heard, you prefer to that of Chriſt, might have informed you better. He replied, " You are in the right !"

I left him Jeruſalem's Meditations *, which he promiſed to read with attention, and took my leave of him, moved and in tears on account of his miſery. He deſired me to viſit him ſoon again.

The third Conference. March the fifth.

WHEN I came to the Count, I addreſſed him thus,—My heart tells me that we ſhall advance to-day a ſtep forwards. I ſee you read Jeruſalem's Meditations. How far are you advanced, and how do you like the book ? " I

* *Conſiderations on the principal Truths of Religion.* To his Highneſs the Hereditary Prince of Brunſwic. Vol. i. Third Edition. *Brunſwic.* 1770.

am

am come already to that meditation which con-cerns the morality of man. The book is ex-cellently written, and I find nothing which contradicts my reafon. I found fomething againft my opinion of man's being a machine; but ftill I think fenfibility proves it, and explains every thing." I anfwered, that the organs of our fenfes were no more than mirrours and fpy-glaffes, through which we obferved the objects; that neither mirrour nor fpy-glafs could fee any thing; but there muft be a third, who obferved the ob-jects through thefe inftruments, and this third was our foul.

He was fenfible of this, but it feemed to be a hard matter for him to own he was in the wrong. Neverthelefs, it was neceffary he fhould make this confeffion before I could proceed any farther. I undertook therefore to prove, that the manner in which his opinion had taken its origin, and had interefted his heart fo much, tended neither to his credit nor to his advantage. I looked upon this as the beft means to expel one fhame by an-other.—He interrupted me very feldom during the time I was fpeaking, but heard with much attention, and owned that I had exactly pointed out the way which had led him to his opinion. After a fhort paufe on both fides, during which he feemed to be in a deep meditation, he called

C

out :

out: " Oh ! I hope now, and wifh for immortality." I gueffed directly that the reading of
Jerufalem had brought him fo far, and he foon
afterwards faid himfelf; " It is impoffible not to
be brought over by that book."

As he now hoped and wifhed for immortality,
I thought it needlefs to enter into more ample
difquifitions about the exiftence, nature and immortality of the foul. Befides, I was afraid that
thefe fpeculative truths might detain us too long,
and miflead us to various refearches which are
but little adapted to make the heart better. It
was enough for me that he now'was fenfible of
the exiftence of eternity : however, we talked
to-day about the arguments for the exiftence of
a foul.

The falfe eafe, which hitherto had rendered the
Count infenfible, and which was fupported by
his perfuafion of there being no future life, was
now interrupted. I thought it neceffary to remove it entirely before I could procure him true
eafe of mind. I muft convince him therefore,
that in that future life, which he hoped and
wifhed for, he could not promife himfelf an
agreeable fate ; and for this purpofe his notions
of the morality of actions were to be rectified
firft. My readers will recollect that he believed

human

human actions only fo far good or bad as they were attended with good or bad confequences to foçiety. Before I could attack this propofition, I thought proper to fhew how little, even according to this principle, he fhould be able to account for his actions before God. I might at prefent, faid I, leave your rule by which you judge of the morality of actions unmolefted. Your actions even then would not bear fcrutiny. I was furprized when he anfwered :

" I find now, that it is by far better and furer to derive the motives of our actions from God, and to confider him as obferving them."

Saying this, he pointed at Jerufalem's book, and I thanked in my heart this excellent man that he had promoted my endeavours fo far.

In the mean time, I begged of the Count to reflect how immoral his actions had been, even according to his former principle of morality. I had now difcovered that fide where the wounds of his confcience fmarted moft. He was not by far fo much grieved at thinking that he had offended God, and made himfelf miferable, as that he had ruined his friends with him. This fenfation of his I laid hold on, and endeavoured to fupport and to increafe it. I hoped his pain

might

.might by degrees become more univerſal, and extend itſelf over his other crimes.

I had ſcarcely began to touch him on this ſide, when he burſt into tears, and owned, that he found himſelf in this reſpect very culpable, and was abſolutely at a loſs to ſay any thing in his defence.

Suppoſe then, continued I, you had to reproach yourſelf only with being the cauſe of all the misfortunes your friends now labour under, it muſt even then be very difficult or rather impoſſible to account for it before God.

" I acknowledge this," ſaid he, " and therefore ſhall ſay nothing to excuſe myſelf before God, and I hope he will not demand this of me. I truſt in my repentance and his mercy. Do not you think God will forgive me on account of this philoſophical repentance?"

According to my notions of repentance, I can give you no hopes. I know but one way to receive God's pardon, and this is not a philoſophical but a Chriſtian repentance. I cannot yet produce the reaſons why I am obliged to think ſo; but if you only reflect on God's mercy, in which you truſt, you will find that it is this very mercy which makes it neceſſary for him to be juſt, and to ſhew his averſion to moral evil.

evil. Such mercy as that of God, which cannot degenerate into weaknefs, muft no doubt be very terrible to him who has offended againft it. I entreat you not to put a blind and ill-founded confidence in it.——Perhaps I pronounced this with a vifible emotion of heart, for he interrupted me, faying, " Your humanity muft be very great, fince your patience is not tired."

It certainly fhall not be tired, but I am uneafy and in pain about you.

" You muft not be fo much concerned for me. ――What would you do if I was fo unhappy as to remain unconvinced ?"

It would grieve me unfpeakably. I fhould wifh to conceive good hopes of you, but I fear without reafon. Pray do what lies in your power, God will blefs your endeavours. I hope you will even yet, upon good grounds, think yourfelf pardoned by God, and be able to die with comfort and a fair profpect into eternity Here he called out, with a deep-fetched figh : " May God grant it !"

He added, " You wifh, and I believe from good reafons, that I might become a Chriftian."

To be fure, (replied I) I wifh it very much ; but you know favours are not forced upon any body ; and it is natural for you to look out for the

greateft

greateſt that can be beſtowed upon you. Learn firſt to feel how dangerous your condition is, and your own wants and miſery will then compel you to ſearch for God's mercy, where it is only to be found.

" But pray," ſaid he, " how can chriſtianity be the only way that is revealed by God for our everlaſting happineſs, ſince it is ſo little known among mankind, and ſince there are, even among chriſtians themſelves, ſo few that keep its precepts ?"

From your firſt doubts, ſaid I, you mean to draw the inference, that it was againſt the goodneſs and juſtice of God not to reveal to all men a doctrine which is the only one that can render man perfectly happy. But do you know whether God will not ſave thoſe who are ignorant of chriſtianity by its diſpenſations, if they behave as well as lies in their power ? And can a man, whom God has preſented with a bleſſing, which he denied to others, think himſelf for this reaſon intitled not to mind this bleſſing or not to value it, becauſe God has not given it to all men ? Has he not diſtributed all the bleſſings of his mercy unequally among men ; for inſtance, honour, riches, health, talents, and even the knowledge of natural religion ? You ſee by

this

this that your objection proves more than you intended.

From your second doubt you will conclude, that, because christianity is observed by so very few, therefore it cannot be a sufficient means to answer the purpose, it is said, God intended it for, and consequently its origin cannot be a divine one. But I would wish you to observe, that it is a religion of free beings, and that they are under no controul in a matter which concerns their happiness. Besides, prejudices, errors and passions can render the strongest moral arguments ineffectual. However, it cannot be denied that mankind, upon the whole, since the establishment of the christian religion, has been greatly reformed, and that its power over the human mind is stronger than you seem to credit.

" But even good christians," added he, " often commit sins! Shall, or can a man in this world be perfect? and is the intention of christianity to produce effects, which, as to our present condition, are quite impossible?"

There is a great difference between the sin of a true christian, of whom we speak only, and between the crimes of a wicked man. The former falls but he rises again; the latter continues in his transgressions and repeats them.

. And

And if there was but one chriftian only upon the whole earth, whofe life did honour to his profeffion, it would be a fufficient reafon for every one that knew him, to examine the religion of this only chriftian, and to adopt it when he found it was well-grounded. He faid: "Oh! I have fo many of thefe doubts, that it will be the moft difficult thing to fatisfy them all."

He uttered this with a mien that expreffed great concern, and I thought proper to comfort him by faying, that his doubts would leffen according as he got more acquainted with chriftianity. And if there fhould be left an uncertainty about fome point or other, he might reft fatisfied with thinking that God would judge him, according to the time he had had, the condition he was in, and the fincerity he fhewed in his fearching after truth; chriftianity concerned more the heart than the underftanding.—I difcovered a hope that he foon would become a chriftian, which he feemed to be pleafed with, and when I exhorted him to pray to God to enlighten his mind, he afked:

" Whether a hearty wifh, addreffed to God, was not already prayer or adoration?"

I anfwered in the affirmative; and after fome exhortations took my leave, and gave him the book
of

of Reimarus *on the principal doctrines of natural religion.*

The fourth Conference. March the eighth.

I HAD now already great advantages in my hands. The Count was fenfible of an approaching eternity, and could not, nor would he any more oppofe the impreffions which the profpect of it made upon him. He was concerned about his moral condition, but not enough yet; at leaft, not on account of the difpleafure of God, which he was labouring under. He wifhed chriftianity might comfort him, but he thought it ftill an impoffibility to be fully convinced of its truth. I now endeavoured to make chriftianity neceffary to him, for reafons which were derived from the mifery and danger he was in. I intended to give him opportunity from time to time, to get acquainted with the arguments of the chriftian religion; that in the fame meafure, as his defire increafed after its comforts, the difficulties which he expected to meet with, might decreafe. But, before I could make him truly fenfible of the danger which his immoral life had thrown him into, we had firft to agree about the reafons, which the morality of human actions is grounded upon.

Since

Since the Count now believed immortality, and in some respect, the morality of actions likewise, I undertook to convince him that human actions are not good or bad, merely on account of their consequences in society, which hitherto had been his opinion.

The reading of the seventh of Jerusalem's Meditations, which treats on the morality of human actions, had, as the Count himself owned, already removed many of his doubts, and taught him that true moral liberty did not consist in determining oneself according to the first impression a thing had made upon us, but that it is required to consider a matter properly, and not to chuse a thing before we are sufficiently acquainted with it. I shewed him, how impossible it was for man always to foresee and to regulate the consequences of his actions, on account of the infirmity and narrow bounds of our understanding, and because we are so easily blinded by our passions.

As to this last reason, the Count himself said, " That passions would overpower us, even then, when we see that the actions to which they excite us can be detrimental to society. They would persuade us, that the consequences they might be attended with are in our power; that by precaution and acting secretly, we might avoid them.

them. They would fupply us with various ex-cufes, and incline us to think them to be true." He did not take it amifs, when I applied this to his own life.

I afterwards proved, that the will of God is the only rule by which the morality of actions is to be determined; not becaufe God had ordered that this action or another fhould be abfolutely good or bad, but becaufe his infinite underftanding found them really fo from all eternity, even without regard to men, created with liberty to trefpafs againft his moral laws.

The next point I thought neceffary to be proved was, that God had really revealed his will about the morality of actions. I would not draw my arguments from the Bible, fince I had not yet proved it to be a divine revelation, but rather from the dictates of confcience.

This being done, as well as the nature of the propofition would admit of, I anfwered the ob-jections which the Count made. The firft was, " That though he had no inclination for raifing any doubts, but fhould rather endeavour to avoid them ; yet the fincerity wherewith our confer-ences were to be carried on, required him to tell plainly, what he was not convinced of. Therefore, he owned, that notwithftanding there

was

was such moral sensation in man, he nevertheless was uncertain, whether it was born with him. Perhaps it might be a certain prejudice?"

If this was so, replied I, how could it happen that this prejudice was an universal one, common both to the virtuous and the wicked?

" Perhaps then," said he, " it is the effect of experience or custom, that we are used to consider the actions of others, as relating to ourselves." My answer was, that this moral sensation is found in man, before he is taught it by experience and custom.

" And suppose," said the Count, " we should find it a consequence of education?"

Neither can this be, replied I, for it is in a child prior to education. It is to be met with in a savage Greenlander and a Hottentot, who reasons on some actions more soundly than nations, whose moral sensations are tainted by education, and by their way of living.

" He now owned, that the notion of morality was born with us, and that it laid deep in our nature. That it took its origin from our Creator, and that we, by the dictates of this inward feeling, were informed of the will of God in regard to good or bad actions."

From

From what he had faid, I now drew fome inferences, and told him, that in order to qualify himfelf for God's mercy, it was neceffary to fearch his former life, and to acknowledge his faults and crimes. I was afraid to leave this felf-examination entirely to himfelf; and therefore told him, that I fhould review with him his life, tho' it was a difagreeable tafk for both; hoping he would affift me therein with all fincerity. He promifed to confefs every thing, and giving me his hand, he faid, he would take me entirely for his guide.

After fome filence on both fides, and amidft his tears, he looked at me with an air that betrayed both anxiety and confidence, and faid, " If my tears come only out of the right fource!"

Good Count, faid I, I fufpect the reafon why you cry. It is certainly the misfortune which you have thrown your friends into. This is your tender fide, which pains, even when it is but flightly touched. Examine yourfelf, whether it is but perfonal friendfhip, or the remembrance of mutual enjoyed pleafures, or the forrow of having loft the hope of their continuation? or, whether it is the confcioufnefs that you have offended God, religion and virtue, in the perfons of your unfortunate friends.

He

He confidered a while, and at laft called out:
" Oh! it is extremely difficult, to come to any
certainty in this point!"

Not long after, he added: " I fear it is now
too late to beg for God's mercy! and perhaps I do it in my prefent fituation out of neceffity!"

I told him upon this, that though he had reafon to reproach himfelf very much, that he had
fpent his whole life without thinking of God, or
endeavouring to make him his friend; yet there
was no diftinction betwixt thofe that came early
and thofe that came late.. It was only the fincerity
with which we feek for God's mercy.

He added, " Perhaps I do it out of complaifance to you." To which I replied, that I
could fcarce believe this, becaufe he fhed fo
many tears, and was fo forry and fo much concerned.

After fome confideration, he faid: " Of what
ufe would it be to me? No, (here he took me by
the hand,) it is not out of complaifance to you."
He then faid: " I remember that in the inftruction
of chriftianity, which I received in my younger
days, I was told, a chriftian ought to die with
the utmoft chearfulnefs and confidence. But I
am fo anxious about doubts. They return al-

ways

ways again, notwithstanding I endeavour to re-move them, and will not let them gain ground."

I suspected, and found afterwards but too justly, that he was throwing out a hint about some strange inward feelings, which some christi-ans pretend to have, as indisputable signs and con-sequences of their being pardoned before God. I therefore told him, that such inward feelings, if there ever were things of that kind, could not be looked upon, as absolutely neceffary, and as things which muft inevitably follow. I knew many fincere chriftians that were without them ; and I myfelf, though confcious of being a chri-ftian, had never perceived them.

He interrupted me, by faying : " I myfelf faw a pious man dying, who left this world in great anxiety."

I continued, Good Count, that eafe of mind which I wifh you, when you are dying, and which it is poffible you may attain, does not con-fift in a vifible joy ; it is rather a certain tran-quillity of the foul, which arifes from a conviction, that we have fulfilled all thofe conditions which God has laid down as the only ones for our receiving his pardon.

" How tottering," faid he, " has been my former fyftem, and how fure was I, neverthelefs,

of

of its truth! I was refolved, that if I fhould die, I would adhere to my principles; I would fuppofe them to be indifputable, and would let death approach without any further fcrutiny. And for this very reafon, I had begged to be excufed from feeing any clergyman."

You fee from this, good Count, replied I, what a difference there is between truth and error. What you mentioned, were your fentiments about eight days ago. And now you read Jerufalem's work with the greateft affiduity, though he contradicts your principles every where.

"Oh!" faid he, "it is an incomparable book; pray bring me the other volumes." How forry was I, that then only one volume was publifhed. "Could you not," continued he, "give this book to be read by fome of my friends, who think of religion as I did, and were perhaps induced to it by my example and converfation?" I promifed I would look out for fuch opportunities.

I now wanted to conduct him further into chriftianity, with whofe moral fide he was to be firft made acquainted; for, as to the dogmatical part he knew already more of it, though he thought it impoffible to believe its myfteries. However, I was fure, that even here, he would become,

become a believer, if he was firft convinced of the
excellency of the morals Chrift has preached, and
if the myfteries of chriftianity were laid before
him, as Scripture propofes them, feparated from
human explications.   To make him converfant
with the precepts of the Gofpel, I thought it beft
to let him read the hiftory of Chrift. I told him,
I wifhed that he might learn from the moral
character of Chrift, that he was a good and divine
man, and one that deferves great credit. Perhaps it may prepoffefs you in his favour, when I
tell you, that even Voltaire, inclined as he is to
calumniate Chrift, does juftice to his moral character. " Does he?" replied the Count. I will
read to you, continued I, fome paffages from the
Evangile du jour, which no doubt is a work of
Voltaire. I added, that Rouffeau was quite
charmed with Chrift's morals, and his death. He
remembered to have found fomething of this
kind in his *Emile*. I might recommend to you,
continued I, the New Teftament, to read the
hiftory of Chrift; but I chufe to decline this at
prefent, fince it is difperfed through all the four
Evangelifts, and fince many places are wrongly
tranflated, and many more, on account of their
reference to the manners of the times and people,
and the fituation of places, might be obfcure to
you; and fince you yourfelf, probably, have

D

abufed

abufed fome Scripture expreffions, to ridicule and to make a jeft of them. " Yes," faid he, " you are in the right." I promifed therefore, to bring to him the hiftory of the three latter years of the life of Chrift, as it is properly compiled, regulated, explained, and told in a modern ftile.

Cramer * had defired me to give his compliments to the Count, and to tell him, that Count Bernftorf had forgiven him, and that he, in the latter days of his life, was very much concerned about the falvation of *his* foul.   He afked: " Has Bernftorf lived to hear of my being arrefted ?" Yes, faid I, he died about a fortnight ago.   He burft out into tears again, and defired me to tell Cramer, that he wifhed to be worthy of his memory, and that he was obliged to him for his intelligence.

I left him to-day Gellert's Lectures on Morality †. He had almoft finifhed Reimarus's book. During my abfence, he always employed the greateft part of his time in reading thofe books which I had brought him.

---

* This eminent divine is now living at Lubeck. He was formerly chaplain at the court of Copenhagen.

† Thefe *Lectures on Morality*, read in the univerfity of Leipfic, *by the late Mr. Gellert*, were tranflated laft year into French. See the Appendix to the 47th volume of the Monthly Review, page 508.

The fifth Conference. March the tenth.

I FOUND the Count reading Gellert's Lectures on Morality, about whofe excellency he did not know how to exprefs himfelf properly. He faid :

" Had I but a year ago read fuch books in retirement from diffipation, I fhould have been quite another man. But I lived as in a dream. However, where are fuch chriftians as are here defcribed?"

I told him that I believed Gellert himfelf to have been fuch a chriftian as is defcribed in the book, which was chiefly written, to fhew that perfection a chriftian was to ftrive for. I reminded him of our agreement, to examine more minutely his moral conduct, in order to convince him more of the greatnefs of his fins, and the neceffity of his repentance.

In a ferious exhortation, I begged of him to act now with all fincerity ; and the Count then began :

" I know very well that I cannot apologize for my actions. But for this very reafon I wifh the exiftence of eternity, becaufe God, who knows exactly the complication of circumftances and the fituation I have been in, will determine more

truly

truly and juftly the morality or immorality of my actions, than men ever can do."

I now delineated the outlines of his character as I had reafon to think it to be. God, faid I, has given you not a common underftanding, and, as I believe, a good natural difpofition of heart; but through voluptuoufnefs, ambition and inconfiderateness, you have corrupted yourfelf. He confirmed my conjectures, and added :

" That voluptuoufnefs had been his chief paffion, which had contributed moft to his moral depravity."

We will begin, faid I, with this paffion, and fee to what fins it has led you. After defcribing how far it was extravagant, the Count owned with great emotion of heart,

" His opinion had always been, that he lived for no other purpofe but to procure himfelf agreeable fenfations. He had reduced every thing to this point, and if now and then he had done fomething good, he had never confidered it as an obligation of charity or of obedience towards God, but as a mere means to promote his own pleafure. In his very youth, he blindly had abandoned himfelf to all forts of extravagancies. When he found the confequences of his irregular life, he endeavoured

to reftore his health again by regularity and continence, in order to enjoy pleafure the longer.
Having recovered health again, he indulged
himfelf in irregularities of voluptuoufnefs under a
mild government of reafon, and refrained himfelf
from abandoned extravagancies. What humiliated
him moft, was, that he could not accufe any body
that had feduced him, but that he muft confefs
to have been his own feducer, by reading certain
books, which he mentioned."

The more minute examination of his life in
regard to this chief paffion of his, I regulated
according to certain queftions. During the whole
enquiry, he did not leave off crying. It feemed
as if he felt a kind of eafe, by intrufting me with
the anxiety of his heart which he felt on account
of this fpecies of tranfgreffion. I will write the
queftions down in the manner I propofed them
to him, and add thofe of his anfwers, which are
more than a fimple confeffion, and can contribute to clear up his former way of thinking, and
ferve to increafe the abhorrence of the vice of
lewdnefs.

How much time has by your eager purfuit of
pleafures been fquandered away, that might and
fhould have been employed better ?—He gave for
anfwer,

D 3" I always

" I always impofed upon myfelf by thinking, becaufe I could work very quick, and could difpatch the bufinefs of my different ftations in life in lefs time than many others, that therefore the reft of my time ought to be dedicated to my pleafures, and was in a manner gained. But I fee now too late, how much it was my duty to be officious in promoting good, according to that meafure of talents God has trufted me with."

How many good actions are left undone? and how infatiable have you been in your luft? How much have you meditated to procure yourfelf new fenfual enjoyments?

" To be overloaded with pleafures, is attended with an inevitable emptinefs, and to fill up the vacancies makes us ftudy variety of pleafures."

How much did you neglect by this the improving and forming of your foul and heart? Remember the years you have fpent at fchool and the univerfity!

" It kept me very backward, and not till late years did I begin to make myfelf acquainted with thofe things which I fhould have learnt at fchool. Being at the univerfity, I lived now and then for whole months together in diffipation and extravagancies, but then I kept to my ftudies for a time again. Improving and forming my heart,

I never

I never thought of before I was two or three and twenty years of age. Since that time I collected by degrees thofe principles of morality I informed you of."

How neglectful has your luft made you to-wards God, yourfelf, and other men, even in thofe duties which your particular ftation in life required of you ?

" I turned my thoughts very little towards God, and did not believe that I owed him any thing more, than a general gratitude for my ex-iftence. I might perhaps have often neglected the particular duties of my refpective ftations in life, for the fake of enjoying pleafures, but at other times I have as phyfician taken great pains about my patients."

Very likely you have, by the perpetual enjoy-ment of fenfual pleafures, heated your fancy, and filled it with foul images, which perhaps difturb you ftill, and hinder your ferious reflexi-ons. In what a giddinefs of luft have you lived, or rather not lived, but only dreamt ?

" When I now recollect, I find that my life has been but a dream. I remember to have done but little good, by which I might know that I really have lived."

How

How much has your luſt degraded your dignity as a man, and ranked you among irrational creatures, whoſe pleaſures conſiſt only in that which is ſenſual ?

" I thought myſelf no more than an animal, and believed there was no difference of ſpecies, but only of ſome degree of perfection between man and beaſt."

Has not your character ſuffered very much by this ?

" I always thought I need not to care what the world ſaid. I therefore endeavoured to pleaſe but a few.   But now I find how valuable a name is which is obtained by virtue."

How indifferent has this made you towards moral pleaſures, which are the moſt effectual ſprings to promote virtue, and are an eſſential part of real happineſs ?

" In my younger years I was quite indifferent towards good ſentiments and actions. Afterwards, though I was perhaps pleaſed when I had done ſomething which I thought to be good, yet I never made any diſtinction between this nobler joy, and the gratification of my luſtful deſires."

How many has your voluptuouſneſs ruined !—
Your example, and the propagating of your
prin-

principles, has seduced young men to profligacy. Many of them have loft their characters, ruined their conftitution, and even met death in their purfuit of luftful pleafures. Perhaps deftitute widows and orphan children, whofe hufbands and fathers were killed by profligacy which you taught them, are now crying to the all-knowing God againft the author of their misfortunes!

He acknowledged, in a very repenting manner, he might be guilty of all thefe crimes. His expreffions, his countenance, and his whole attitude feemed to beg of me not to go on any further. I continued:

Might you not have been the feducer of innocent young women, and might you not, on fuch occafions, have wilfully facrificed to your voluptuoufnefs, religion, honour, and virtue? Might you not have ruined them in this world, by hindering their being married, and throwing them into contempt and poverty?

" I cannot deny that I have been a dangerous feducer. I often have deceived innocence by my principles. Even women of good fenfe I have conquered; and more than this, I have made them afterwards eafy again about their tranfgreffions. None among thofe that I attacked was at laft able to refift me, if fhe did not avoid

me

me prefently. I was never at a lofs how to conquer; though I muft fay, I never promifed any
thing which I did not intend to perform. Notwithftanding I did all that laid in my power to
keep thofe, who through my fault had been tem-
porally ruined, from mifery and poverty, I am,
neverthelefs, now convinced that this by no
means can excufe me."

Perhaps there are children that do not know
you to be their father, who for want of education
will become a burden to fociety, and are in danger of being ruined in this and the future world.

Here he defired me to take upon me the care
and education of a child, two years old, becaufe
it was his.

I fcarcely had made enquiry, when I heard it
was dead. I mention this as a proof of his fincerity. I continued:

And matrimonial ties, which according to the
unanimous opinion of all nations fhould be facred, I fuppofe you have broken. What an
irreparable injury is hereby done to both parties!
—and how much muft this injuftice have afflicted the injured party? Remorfe of confcience on
the fide of the feduced perfons was or will be the
confequence thereof. Wherewith will you excufe
yourfelf, if grief or defpondency fhould be hurt-

ful

ful to the health or the life of the injured ? Is not matrimonial happinefs and domeftic peace fre-quently difturbed by thefe your tranfgreffions ?

" The injured party, faid he, had often never known of it, and in fome inftances he had rather promoted domeftic peace by good advice, which he had given to the female criminal. He owned that he thought thefe excufes formerly fufficient, but he did not mention them now with the fame intent."

Perhaps, faid I, honeft fathers are obliged to maintain children, which they are convinced are not their own. Of what confufions, enmities, and law-fuits may this be productive, even after your death, in families that might have remained happy, if you had left them undifturbed ? Have you never ufed unnatural means to fatisfy your voluptuous paffions, or to prevent their difagree-able and unexpected confequences ? He faid:

" In his younger years he had indulged him-felf in every thing his paffion had driven him to, but as to the latter part of the queftion, he knew himfelf to be innocent."—And this was the only accufation of our to-day's fcrutiny, to which he pleaded not guilty.

Now, continued I, what mifery have all thefe extravagancies thrown you into? Forget for a

little

little while that you have offended God extremely, by creating fo much mifchief in the world. Reflect rather on this queftion only, How has **my** luftful paffion rewarded me, after having ferved it fo faithfully? You are rewarded with tranfitory, difguftful joys, which never have fatisfied your defires; with difdain, contempt, and reproaches of all fober people that knew of your wicked life; with imprifonment and fetters, with a premature and ignominious death.——Pray now, confider ferioufly, fuppofe I and every body were to live in this manner, what would become of human fociety?——He anfwered,

" I foolifhly perfuaded myfelf, that it was confiftent with fociety. The great ones in England and France, faid I to myfelf, lead fuch unreftrained life."

But, faid I, does this unreftrained way of life of the great in England and France contribute towards the happinefs of either nation? And can it be believed that they, in doing fo, are more happy than people of the middle fort, that lead a life which is more ftrict and more folid? And laftly, are thefe great ones the whole fociety, or are they not the fmalleft part of it, and if numbers are to be confidered, the moft inconfiderable part?

During

During the whole time of this converſation, the Count was very much moved, and ready to cry. I ſaw how affecting and humiliating the ſcene of his paſt life was to him.

" How is it poſſible, ſaid he, that I could ever be ſo convinced of my former principles, and could ever forget myſelf ſo far !"

I recommended to him to ſearch the whole courſe of his former life more minutely, and left him for this purpoſe further written inſtructions. I gave him likewiſe the two firſt parts of the three laſt years of the life of Chriſt. The Count then ſaid:

" That he valued the morals of chriſtianity very much, and thought them truly divine; but he was afraid the myſteries of religion might prevent his being fully perſuaded of its truth, though he promiſed to ſpare no pains to get convinced."

Upon this I told him, that the grace of God would aſſiſt his endeavours, and that his doubts would ceaſe in time. He then ſtarted three objections: the firſt, why the immortality of the ſoul was not taught in the writings of Moſes? the ſecond, how Chriſt could be the Son of God? and thirdly, how three perſons could be in one Deity? To the firſt I replied, that if it was agreed

that

that in the writings of Mofes no mention was made of the immortality of the foul, it did nevertheless by no means follow, that this doctrine was unknown to the Jews, or that the truth of it was lefs certain. And as for his fecond and third objections, I told him, that fince their refutation is grounded upon right explanations of fcripture paffages, for which he was not yet prepared, I could only tell him this beforehand, that the words wherein thefe myfteries are revealed, muft be cautioufly explained, fince they were more adapted to inform men of the exiftence of what is above their conception, than to exprefs fully the nature of the myftery.

The fixth Conference. March the twelfth.

I Now conducted the Count to the fecond great fource of his tranfgreffion, which, I thought, was his ambition. You had, faid I, too great an opinion of your underftanding, and of the goodnefs of your intentions, which at the bottom were but means to fatisfy your chief paffion. He replied :

" He had been fo weak, as to let himfelf be perfuaded by a perfon that made too much of him, that his underftanding was fo great, that he
                                        could

could do every thing which was in the power of man.. Helvetius, whom he had read much, had likewife induced him to believe this. For he fays, that fince the organifation of every man was the fame, confequently every one was capable of doing the fame thing another man could do. He had thought himfelf convinced of the goodnefs of his intentions, though he muft own he had purfued principles which ought to be rejected, and that always the chief end he had in view was his pleafure."

I then put him in mind how many people he had made unhappy through his ambition; how unjuft and hard he had been to fatisfy this paffion; how obftinately he oppofed thofe that underftood the affairs of ftate better than himfelf, even then when he knew he was in the wrong. What dangerous and violent means he had ufed to keep himfelf in his dignity, and to what danger he had expofed the fubjects of the King, particularly the inhabitants of the metropolis. To this he replied,

" It was true, that he for his own fafety had made regulations which he had not thought to be dangerous, fince he knew inftances wherein even the fight only of fuch preparations had prevented and quelled difturbances. But now, when he confi-

confidered matters more coolly, he faw very well that he might have been the author of great mif-chief."

I defired him to confider, whether he had not made too free with the revenues of the ftate ?—At how great an expence he had lived at laft ?—What an unconftitutional power he had arrogated to himfelf? &c.

The two chief paffions of the Count, voluptuoufnefs and ambition, being accompanied with great inconfideratenefs, I reminded him of his inconfiderate treatment of religion, and how he had made a jeft of the moft ferious things in the world, and ftudied perhaps to communicate his opinions to others. To which he gave for anfwer :

" He could not deny that religion had frequently been with him a fubject of ridicule. But he had been guilty of this kind of inconfideratenefs, moftly in the company of fuch perfons as were already prejudiced againft religion. He never had made it his bufinefs to make profelytes, though he had made no fecret of his irreligion. He acknowledged himfelf in all this culpable before God and his confcience."

After feveral other queftions, I afked the Count how he could prefume to fit at the helm of

3

government,

government, when he knew himfelf by no means qualified for it, being without knowledge of the laws, and the language of the country, and never giving himfelf the trouble to learn either. I charged him with having given new laws inconfiderately, abolifhing old ones without reafon. I blamed him for having difcharged old and approved of minifters of ftate, and chufing new ones, without knowing them, and trufting in them without being fure of their being honeft men; only becaufe he thought they would prove themfelves to be his friends.

When I told him, that he never had cared for the morals of the nation, but rather promoted immorality by bad examples, by giving opportunities to do evil, and even by making laws tending to promote it, he faid:

" He always believed, that it belonged only to the clergy to mind the morals of the people. He judged of the fentiments of the nation by his own, and imagined that every one, like himfelf, looked upon pleafure and an unreftrained life as the only happinefs."

When I reprefented to him, that during his adminiftration there was, efpecially in the metropolis, an entire ftop to trade, he replied:

E" He

" He had been senfible of that, and it was no matter of indifference to him, for he had been thinking how to open new ways to promote trade."

When I afked him how it was poffible for him to fee the univerfal difcontent, and to be fenfible of it, to be cautioned by friends and foes, and neverthelefs to neglect all this, he anfwered :

" He had always made himfelf eafy, **by the** hopes that this difcontent would ceafe at laft, and that the meafures he had taken would keep him fafe."

Though all thefe reproaches were fevere and very humiliating, the Count feemed, neverthelefs, not to be offended by them. Now and then he would fay fome things in his excufe, which were nothing to me, becaufe they did not relate to what I had in view, and which I was not a judge of. However, he was upon the whole full of repentance, though he thought he could apologize for fome particular parts of his political conduct.

" He expreffed his anxiety, that he thought his repentance was not ferious enough, or at leaft that he was more forry on account of fome tranf-greffions than others."

I anfwered,

I answered, this fear of his was a good sign, and a proof of the sincerity of his repentance. I reminded him of God's mercy towards him, since in his prison he had time and opportunity to consider his former actions, and to repent of his crimes. I asked what might have become of him, if an assassination had taken place, which he was so often threatened with, and which so easily could have been put into execution?

Since the last conference, the Count had read the two first parts of the history of Christ, and I enquiring how he liked *the man?* he said:

" His morals and his personal conduct are excellent. The first are undoubtedly the best advice for men to make themselves happy in all situations of life. Here and there I found something which I did not understand, and which perhaps is to be explained from the manners and condition of those times. But I have met with many things that have affected me much. It has humiliated me to find here many good things, which I had learned in my youth from Scripture, and which I afterwards believed I owed to the reading of other books."

When I enquired of him, if it was likely that a man whose life and morals were so excellent, and who acted so disinterestedly (" and, as he

                              added

added himself, who facrificed his life to confirm the truth of what he preached") was capable of impofing upon the world by falfe miracles, he anfwered :

' " No ! it is quite improbable."

I then told him that there are two ways to get convinced of the truth of the chriftian religion. The firft and the more fure one, was a conftant practice of Chrift's precepts. By this a man may be convinced by his own experience of the excellency of his religion. The other was, a candid examination whether Chrift had proved himfelf to be a true meffenger of God, by delivering a doctrine which was worthy of God, and by performing undoubted miracles. As to the doctrine, he had owned already that it was really divine; and if the greateft of his miracles, his refurrection, could be proved, it followed in courfe, that the reft of his miracles were true, or at leaft could be fo. I told him it was neceffary for him to examine the evidences in behalf of this miracle himfelf; and for this purpofe I fhould give him a book which was written by a deift, who was induced to turn chriftian after examining the refurrection of Chrift.

The Count feemed to be greatly pleafed by this; and I left him with fanguine hopes, after
I had

I had given him the third and fourth parts of the Life of Chrift.

The feventh Conference. March the fourteenth.

GEneral Lieutenant Holben, the commander of the caftle where the Count was prifoner, told me, that fince my laft vifit he had been very uneafy: That he frequently on a fudden ftarted from the couch upon which he ufed to lie during the whole time of his imprifonment: That he had been fitting for half an hour together, hanging down his head, buried in deep thoughts, and fobbing had fhed a great many tears. When I entered the prifon, I found him reading Gellert, and reading indeed I always found him whenever I came.

" I muft be quite deprived of all my reafon, faid he, if I did not own, that I fhould have lived as this book teaches me. Oh! had I but read fuch books in the days of my profperity, I am fure they would have convinced and reformed me."

His countenance expreffed great concern, fhame and uneafinefs. And when I afked him how he did, he replied:

" I am very uneafy fince yefterday. I cannot ferioufly enough repent of having led fo bad a life,

and

and having acted upon such wicked principles, and used means so detrimental. My present condition, and even my death do not concern me so much as my base actions! And it is quite impossible to make any reparation for what I have done to the world.—Pray, my dear friend, do not be tired, and do not leave me."

Though I had the greatest compassion towards him, yet I thought I had not reason enough at present to make him quite composed. But when he seemed to be afraid his repentance might be too late, I comforted him in this respect, and promised to shew myself his friend to the very last. My intention by this visit was to give him opportunities to recollect his former life, and to point out to him the way for a serious repentance; but the uneasiness I found him in, would not allow me to act so seriously as I intended. Among other subjects which we were talking upon, was the pain and grief which he had caused to his honest parents from his earlier days, and now in particular towards the latter end of his life. I entreated him to consider how often he had offended them by his disobedience and obstinacy, and made them grieve about his open contempt of all religion.—What anxiety, continued I, must you have caused to these venerable persons, by those inconsiderate steps you have taken during your refidence in this metropolis!—Every news of the too hafty increafe of their fon's profperity, of the means he got at it, and the ufe he made of his power, muft have ftruck a kind of deadly terror into them!—They muft have trembled every day on account of the danger which threatened their fon; and into what an unfpeak-able grief muft your fudden fall have thrown them!—How dreadful muft their expectation be on account of the iffue of your affairs, and the danger your foul is in!—How humiliating to them will be the manner of your death! Will they ever be comforted, and might it not fhorten their lives? And who is the author of all this? are not you, their fon!

I had had, for feveral days, a letter of the father * of the unfortunate Count in my pocket, and I thought this moment the propereft to deliver it. The whole letter is as follows:

"I could

---

* The accounts which are given in news papers and ma-gazines of the father of Count Struenfee being fo imperfect, and full of mifreprefentations, the tranflator, who is perfo-nally acquainted with him, will give here a fhort fketch of his life. D. Adam Struenfee, the father of the Count, was born in the year 1708, at New Ruppin, a fmall town, in the dominions of the King of Pruffia. He was foon fent to the grammar fchool at Brandenburg, where he was till the year 1727, when he went to the univerfity at Halle, which he ex-changed the following year for that of Jena. In the year 1730 the Count of Witgenftein made him one of his chaplains at Berleburg. He was but one year in this ftation before he

was

" I could wish that these lines, if possible, may reach you, that you may read and consider. The me ancholy, grief, and anxiety of your parents,

on

was chosen rector of a parish in the suburbs of Halle, in Saxony. He quitted this living but a few months after for another rectory in the city of Halle, which he likewise gave up soon after, another living in the same city being offered to him, and of which he accepted. He then was made professor in divinity of the University, in which capacity of professor and rector he got a great name, and became very eminent, and much beloved. In the year 1757, the late King of Denmark gave him the principal rectory at Altona, and appointed him president of the ecclesiastical consistory of Altona and the county of Pinneberg. His talents and merits promoted him in the year 1760 to one of the most eminent preferments in the Lutheran church, for he became president of the ecclesiastical council, general-superintendant (or bishop) of the two dukedoms Schleswig and Holstein, to which are annexed the deanries of Gottorp, Rendsburg, Husum, and Schwabsted. He now, at this very time, enjoys all these preferments, and his fixed residence is at Rendsburg, a fortified town in Holstein, where the translator visited him in the year 1766. He is a very personable, tall man, has a serious countenance, is a good pulpit orator, whose discourses are more calculated for edification than for shining eloquence. He has the promoting of practical religion particularly in view. Many are his writings and publications, which are mostly calculated for the same purpose. He married, in the year 1732, Mary Charles, only daughter of John Charles, then physician in ordinary to the Count of Witgenstein, a lady of singular merit, virtue and piety. It is said, that the fate of her sons affected her so much, that she lately died of grief. She was mother of eight children.

1. Elisabeth, born 1733, and married to a clergyman at Brandenburg.

2. Charles August, born 1735. He was professor of mathematics at Lignitz, in Silesia. His brother, the Count, called him in 1771 into Denmark, and made him counsellor of justice. He was made prisoner of state with his brother, but afterwards set at liberty again. He has published a well written treatise on fortification.

3. John

on account of their fons *, I am not able to exprefs. Our eyes fwim in tears, day and night. Our fouls cry for mercy to God without ceafing. But I will fpeak no more of this. There is but one thing which lies heavy upon my mind, and

that

3. John Frederick, the unhappy Count, whofe name will be recorded in the annals of Denmark, was born the fifth of Auguft, 1737, at Halle. He was educated in the fchools of the famous orphan houfe of D. Franke, and in the univerfity at Halle, where he ftudied phyfic. He went with his father to Altona, where he foon became royal phyfician of the counties of Ranzau and Pinneberg, and procured himfelf by his profeffion and induftry a moderate independency. In the year 1768, the fifth of April, the King of Denmark appointed him to be his phyfician in ordinary, who was to attend him during his travels through Germany, England and France. This laid the foundation of his following profperity. He got intimately acquainted with the young monarch, was always about him, and infinuated himfelf into his particular favour. He was made *Lecteur Royal*, and in 1769, the 12th of May, actual counfellor of ftate. In 1770, the 19th of May, he was appointed counfellor of conference, and *Maitre de requetes*; and in July, 1771, he became prime minifter. The fame month he was raifed to the dignity of a Danifh Count, and the Queen invefted him with the order of Matilda. In 1772, the 17th of January, he became prifoner of ftate, and loft his life the 28th of April.

4. Samuel Adam, born 1739, lives with his father.

5. Mary, born 1744, is married to a clergyman at Shlefwig.

6. Harriet, born 1745, died very young.

7. Chriftian, born 1746.

8. Gothilf, born 1752. He ftudied at Gottingen, but the Count, his brother, called him from thence, and made him lieutenant in the King's guards. He was likewife arrefted, but fet at liberty again under condition of quitting the Danifh dominions.

* It muft be remembered, that two brothers of the Count were likewife arrefted with him.

that of your much afflicted mother. You know our sentiments. You know our intention when we educated you. You remember how often and how seriously we inculcated this great truth, that godliness is profitable unto all things.

As often as I had occasion to speak to you, even then, when you were in a public character, I reminded you of the omni-present God, and exhorted you to be careful in preserving a good conscience. Your own heart will tell you, how far you have lived up to the exhortations of your father.

It is already a long while that your parents have been in great anxiety about you. Since we lead a retired life, and have very few acquaintance, and you yourself have written nothing about your circumstances, the prayers and sighs of our straitened hearts have ascended to God in secret, and in our anxiety we cried, that your soul might not be lost. Three different times, at Haile, Gedern, Altona, you were looked upon as a dead man, by those that stood about your sick bed. God has saved you and preserved your life: Certainly with that only intent, to prepare you in this time of grace for an happy eternity. The same is now the chief intention of your gracious Redeemer, in your prison. You are

his

his creature, he loves you, you are redeemed by the blood of Jefus. God is a reconciled father. You are baptized in the name of the Trinity. He will make an everlafting covenant with you, and he will not defift from doing good to you. Return to your God, my fon, he will not hide his face of grace from you. Mind the voice of your confcience, and the conviction which the Spirit of God produces in your foul. Pray to God that he may difclofe to you the true inward ftate of your foul, that you, enlightened by God, may fee how much you are corrupted. Employ the folitude you are in now, to fearch your whole life in the fight of the all knowing God, that you may fee how great and how deteftable your fins are. Do not flatter yourfelf. Be rigorous with your-felf. Accufe yourfelf and judge yourfelf before the tribunal of God, whilft you are ftill enjoying this time of grace.

When you fhall feel your fins to be a heavy burden, your heart then will humiliate itfelf before God, you will pray for mercy, and you will ferioufly deteft and abhor your tranfgreffions. You then will fee the great importance and neceffity of the redemption of Chrift. You then will take refuge in him who receives finners, who was made to be fin for us, who has paid the debts of our fins, and fuffered their punifhment, that

we

we might be made the righteousnefs of God in him, and might have redemption through his blood, the forgivenefs of fins, according to the riches of his grace. Still the blood of Chrift fpeaks for you. He that is merciful, ftill ftretches forth his hands. Without Jefus there is no falvation. He is the caufe of it. Even for your fake he has received gifts. You may have in him righteoufnefs for your peace of mind and for your fanctification. O that Jefus might be glorified in your heart. In him we have happinefs whilft we live, whilft we fuffer, whilft we die, and after death.

Your mother gives her love to you. She weeps,—fhe prays with me, for our unfortunate fons. My fon, my fon, how deeply do you afflict us! Oh! could we but have this only comfort, that our fons turned with all their heart unto the Lord, and that we with joy might find them again in eternity before the throne of the Lamb!

Your crimes, which brought you into prifon, are not properly and fufficiently known to us. What is talked of and read in public about you, is of fuch a nature that your parents condemn and deteft it. Oh! I wifh to God, you had remained a phyfician. Of your rife to honours we were informed by the news papers; but it was

no

no matter of joy to us; we read it with grief. Oh! that you had kept, in all your tranfactions, a clear confcience with much wifdom, piety, and humility, for the good of Denmark, and that you might have fubmitted with all due fubjection, to all the commands of your Sovereign. We cannot altogether judge about this matter for want of information. But know, that tho' we love our children, we neverthelefs do not approve of their crimes, nor will we excufe or palliate them, or call them good; we rather hate all fins, deteft, condemn, and abhor them, and praife God when he manifefts his juft wrath over the wicked, and fhews his mercy to the repenting and the faithful. The Lord our God be your phyfician in your imprifonment, and cure thoroughly the wounds of your foul.

We your parents recommend you to the love of the Lord that has mercy on you. May Jefus, who is a compaffionate High-prieft, remember you for good at the right hand of God, that you may receive mercy before the throne of grace, and be pardoned unto everlafting falvation. Yea, Jefus! thou great friend of mankind, who wilt in no wife caft out him that comes to thee, help parents and children to life everlafting!"

Rendfburg, March the 4th, 1772.

When I told the Count that I had a letter from his father to him, he took it with a kind of eagernefs, and began to read. But he had not half finifhed it, when he laid it down, weeping bitterly. Looking then at me with an air of confidence, he faid, " It is impoffible for me to read any further; I will begin again by and by."

My anfwer was, Read it by yourfelf, and read it often. It is a letter of an honeft, afflicted, and tender parent. Endeavour to comfort your virtuous father and your pious mother, by a chriftian-like anfwer. You know very well what alone can comfort them.

" Oh ! my God," faid he, in a manner which cannot be expreffed, " I cannot write to them, I do not know how I fhall act !"

You will have time, replied I, to confider about this.—He afterwards praifed his father for being an honeft man, whofe actions agreed with his fentiments, and his mother for being a matron, that deferved reverence and was really pious. He faid, fhe had given him the beft opportunity to learn by her own example, practical chriftianity. He begged of me, " To write foon to his parents, to tell them the whole truth how I found him, and to affure them that he would do his beft, and had the beft intention, to

die

die like a chriftian."—He was fo much affected, that he was fcarcely able to pronounce thefe words.

I had now given him opportunities enough for felf-examination. His repentance was really fincere, and I could truft in it fo much the more, as he was a man of cool blood, and one who, through principles and practice, had obtained great power over his paffions, and who certainly could not have been moved by any thing elfe, but by ferious remonftrances of his confcience. I reminded him of that hope, which he formerly had entertained, that God would fhew him mercy on account of his philofophical repentance. I defired him to tell me whether he thought this ftill to be true? He hardly knew what to anfwer, but at laft, he faid: " I feel it too much, that I have no grounds for fuch a hope. I am no more inclined to deceive myfelf."

I now wanted to make him acquainted with the proofs of chriftianity ; for which purpofe, I had brought him Weft's Obfervations on the Hiftory and Refurrection of Jefus Chrift. I defired him to read with attention. And if he fhould find, that there was the greateft credibility in the hiftory of the refurrection of Chrift, he then fhould afk his reafon, whether he had no obli-

gation

gation to believe him, that was rifen, to be a meffenger of God to men, and his doctrine to be true and divine?

The eighth Conference.   March the 16*th.*

MY firft queftion was: Is it probable that fins fhould be punifhed in a future world which were committed wilfully, which were often repeated, and which were terrible on account of their confequences?

He anfwered, " That if one looked upon it with mere reafon, it fhould feem probable that the uneafinefs of confcience and the natural confequences of fins, were fufficient for their punifhment."

Many reafons being produced on my fide, and among the reft, that many went out of this world without any remorfe of confcience at all; the Count gave his objection up. And when I, at the conclufion of thofe arguments which are in favour of rewards and punifhments, propofed the queftion: Why even a finner who difapproves of all religion, is at leaft then afraid, when he fees certain death before his eyes?

The Count faid: " It might perhaps be nothing elfe but that natural fear of death which

is

is common to all." But he found afterwards this objection removed by his own experience; for he owned he was now lefs afraid on account of his death than of his fins. However, he believed he fhould have died with very little fear, even if we had not got acquainted, and he had not read thofe books I brought him.

When I endeavoured to prove that mere repentance is not fufficient to fatisfy divine juftice refpecting our crimes, and afked what he would think of a judge who fhould pardon every criminal when he fhewed figns of a ferious repentance; he anfwered, " he fhould think him to be a good man though a weak one, who was neither juft nor wife, and unfit to be a judge."

Upon this, I undertook to convince him that mere repentance, or reparation of damages, or reformation of life, were infufficient to expiate our fins before God: I concluded, that thefe three mentioned means, which reafon recommends for obtaining pardon, are infufficient.

I afterwards told the Count, that though he could not repair the damages he had done, becaufe he was fo near eternity, he neverthelefs could ftill do fomething which refembled, in fome refpect, a reparation; and this was, that he fhould endeavour to efface thofe bad impref-

<table><tr><td>F</td><td align="right">fions</td></tr></table>

fions he had made upon the minds of the people, by fhewing himfelf now quite a different man in his converfation and his whole behaviour. The Count affured me, " that he himfelf already had thought this to be his duty. He had fpoken to an officer about the moral doctrines of chrif-tianity, and exhorted him to obey them ftrictly. But he had not fpoken like a fully-convinced chrif-tian, for he was none yet, and he thought he had no right to play the hypocrite." He added, " that he heartily wifhed he could only con-tribute fomething towards the reformation of thofe of his friends, whofe morals and fentiments he had corrupted by his example and by his converfation."

When I had proved that faith in Chrift was the only way for reconciliation, I enquired of him how he had found the evidences of Chrift's refurrection.

" You know," anfwered the Count, " that for fome days paft my mind has been very un-eafy and my body fick. I confefs both have hindered me from reading that part of the book with fufficient attention, which examines and compares the circumftances of the refurrection of Chrift. However I have found in the latter part the following arguments, which have made a

great

great impreffion upon my underftanding. The difciples of Chrift were not credulous, but were with difficulty convinced of the refurrection of Chrift by the unanimous teftimony of all their fenfes. The Jews never examined the affair judicially, though they had the beft opportunity for it, and it was their intereft to fhew it was fictitious. I likewife look upon the propagation of chriftianity as another argument of the truth of Chrift's refurrection; for if it had not been certain that Chrift had rifen, chriftianity could not have fpread fo quick and fo far as it has done. The doctrine of Muhamed is in regard to its propagation not to be compared with chriftianity. However, I could wifh to know, whether any teftimonies for Chrift's refurrection are to be met with in heathen authors."

I told him, that Suetonius, Tacitus, Plinius, and Jofephus made mention of Chrift, though there was a difpute about the paffage of the latter being genuine.

" I cannot deny," faid the Count, " that Chrift's refurrection feems to be probable; but it appears to me a little odd, that he, after his re- furrection, did not fhew himfelf to his enemies."

This objection I endeavoured to remove, by fhewing that fuch a teftimony would have been

of

of no ufe, and would never have convinced the Jews, on account of their obftinacy.

The Count being exhorted to pray, he affured me that he already frequently prayed. And when he repeated his complaint that his repentance on account of fome actions, and in relation to fome perfons, was greater than on account of others, I told him, that this was very natural; that he always would find himfelf more concerned on account of the misfortunes he had brought upon his friends, his parents, his brothers, and Count Brandt.

After fome filence, he faid : " I do not know whether error and paffion might not carry me away a fecond time, in cafe I fhould enter the world again. But fuch as I find myfelf now, I deteft my extravagancies, even thofe which gave me pleafure; and I believe that in cafe I had an opportunity of indulging myfelf again, I fhould not commit them."

When I exhorted him not to commit any wrong action which he was in his prefent circum-ftance capable of doing, and defired him to be upon his guard againft telling any untruth before his judges, or apologizing for himfelf when he had no ground for it, or concealing what was true, he anfwered :

" I know

" I know that by a fincere confeffion, I gain in the opinion of honeft men. I am convinced that all my future happinefs, which I now hope to obtain, would be loft if I fhould attempt to conceal the truth. I even believe, according to the morals of Chrift, that a lie, though told with a good intent of promoting chriftianity and virtue, would be culpable. You therefore may depend upon my telling without referve every thing I fhall think myfelf guilty of."

When I took my leave of him, he faid : " I fee how much you are concerned about my falvation; that you love me, and as a fincere friend want to promote my real good. I look upon you as my only true friend in the world. When fhall I fee you again ? I am longing for you when you are not here ?"—I replied,

The day after to-morrow you will certainly fee me again ; but the nearer the time draws that fhall decide your fate, the more frequently I fhall vifit you, and ftay longer with you.

He fmiled and faid : " I hope you will not fall fick."

I gave him to-day *Bonnet's philofophical Examination of the Arguments of Chriftianity.*

The ninth Conference. March the eighteenth,

I NOW recommended Scripture to the Count. The New Teſtament, ſaid I, gives the moſt perfect information, and the Old Teſtament agrees with the New, particularly in that chief point of man's redemption. I pointed out and explained ſeveral paſſages of the prophets which correſpond with the evangeliſts, and drew the inference, that even this muſt prepoſſeſs us greatly in favour of the truth of the Goſpel hiſtory. The Count replied:

" If one had a mind to entertain ſuſpicion, one might ſay Chriſt had formed himſelf after the character of the Meſſias, as it was drawn by the prophets, to act the part of this great perſonage."

I anſwered: If he had had a mind for doing this, he would have acted his part conſentaneous with the prejudices of the Jews, and appeared in the character of a worldly hero.

" To be ſure, (was his anſwer) he then would have employed quite different means. It is impoſſible for an impoſtor to act thoroughly the part of an honeſt man. Beſides, there are prophecies, which, in regard of their being fulfilled,

did

did not depend entirely upon Chrift. For inftance : the cafting lots over his garments, and his being crucified. One as well as the other depended on accidental circumftances. If the Romans had not been at that time mafters of Jerufalem, he might not have been crucified, but rather been ftoned to death."

We examined hereupon thofe Scripture paffages which treat on the redemption of men by Chrift. I endeavoured to prove that this redemption, as it is taught in Scripture, does not contradict any of God's attributes, but is in all refpects adapted and fuitable to the condition of men.—This being done, after it had taken up much of our time, I entreated the Count moft earneftly to get convinced of this chief doctrine of chriftianity, that there is no falvation without Chrift, and to adopt it for his own everlafting welfare. He faid, " he fhould raife no difficulties, but fhould do as much as he could to get convinced of a doctrine which muft be of fo great importance to him. He had no other hopes but from this quarter only, and why fhould he therefore not be defirous of partaking thereof."

I found him at once greatly moved again. He complained with tears in his eyes—" that

his

his old idea of a total annihilation of our whole existence after death, would return now and then and make him uneasy."

I told him it was very difficult to eradicate old ideas we were formerly so much pleased with: But I hoped he would always get the better of them, if he kept those arguments in view which he had found convincing in those books he had read upon this subject.

He then asked me: "If I never had entertained any doubts about eternity?" No! was my answer; I always found it suitable to my wishes. I got early acquainted with its proofs.

Upon the Count's complaining that he still was afraid his repentance might not be sincere enough; I advised him to do just such actions as were opposite to his former vices, and to mind every opportunity which was left for him of doing good. I said I would propose something to him. The proposal was, that since he was very sorry for having many of his former friends prepossessed against religion by communicating to them his principles, he should renounce these principles publickly. He should give an account to the world of the sentiments in which he intended to die, and of the manner they took place.

" This

" This is what I fhall do," replied he; " I will confider in what manner I could draw this up to make it moft ufeful."—Laftly he wifhed, " that he might have a lively fenfation of the comfort of religion:" He faid, " he prayed heartily to God for it." I told him, God would grant him his wifhes, and it would follow in courfe the more he got convinced of the truth of the chriftian religion, and of the fincerity of the alteration in his fentiments.

He anfwered: " I hope to get convinced. I formerly thought that whoever embraced chriftianity was to renounce all reafon; but I now fee plainly, that nothing ftands more to reafon than chriftianity; and I promife you, that I will do my utmoft to make my fentiments conformable to the will of God."

I then continued: Your mind will grow eafy, and you will feel the comforts of the Gofpel. But, neverthelefs, you may feel anxiety and fear towards the latter end of your life, and upon the way to the fcaffold. I tell you this before-hand, left you may think religion could not comfort us when we are to die. Natural fear of death, the terrifying circumftances your's will be attended with, and your being confcious that you by your crimes brought yourfelf to it, will not

be

be altogether removed. But by the affiftance of religion, you will have a calm and hopeful profpect into eternity.

He had now finifhed Bonnet's book which I had left with him, and declared it had given him great fatisfaction. And fince Rouffeau had been his favorite author, and I feared his objections againft Chrift's miracles might appear to him of confequence, I gave him *Claperede on the miracles of the Gofpel*, to let him fee how weak Rouffeau's objections are againft facts.

The tenth Conference. March the twentieth.

MY intention by this conference was to convince the Count that reafon could make no objections of any confequence againft the doctrine of the redemption of the world by Chrift.

" I myfelf," faid the Count, " have been thinking already on this fubject. Perhaps God will try our intentions towards his precepts, by demanding our faith in favour of this doctrine of redemption. And if this fhould be the cafe, it is a fufficient reafon for us to believe it."

' Hereupon I proved that the doctrine of redemption glorifies the divine perfections, and is

abfoabſolutely neceſſary to human happineſs. At the concluſion of my arguments I entreated the Count to profeſs himſelf a chriſtian by believing in Chriſt. Ceaſe, ſaid I, good Count, to be an unhappy man. Believe in Jeſus, and your ſins will be forgiven you. Your death will open you the door into a bleſſed eternity.

Here enſued a ſcene which was moving to me beyond deſcription. Never felt I ſuch joy. Never have I been ſo ſure of the happineſs of having brought back a ſinner from his errors ! I ſhall never forget this ſolemn and joyful hour, and never ceaſe to praiſe God for it.

" I ſhould be guilty of the greateſt folly," ſaid the Count, " if I would not embrace chriſtianity with joy, when its arguments are ſo over-balancing, and when it breathes ſuch gene-ral benevolence. Its effects upon my heart are too ſtrong. Oftentimes I cannot help crying when I read the hiſtory of Chriſt. I think already with hope on my death. I have acquainted myſelf with its moſt terrifying circumſtances. I do not know how I ſhall be when the awful hour comes. At preſent I am not uneaſy about it; I find nothing that makes me anxiouſly wiſh for this life. I will confidently expect forgiveneſs of my ſins through Chriſt. And to you, my dear friend,

2

friend, I am infinitely obliged that you have brought me so far."

I embraced him, and exhorted him to thank God for it. We prayed together.——

I would now have left him, but he begged of me to stay half an hour longer, which I did.

He complained that his former idea, that there perhaps was no eternity, now and then returned to him; (and in fact it did not leave him entirely until a few days before his death.) He said, with a kind of indignation and grief: " Sometimes I think again ; suppose my former idea was true, that we have no exiftence after death ? But I comfort myfelf by thinking, that I abhor this idea ; and that I am fenfible it would be a very unhappy profpect if all my wifhes and expectations of futurity fhould be vain. I tremble when this melancholy thought difturbs me, and I arm myfelf againft it by recollecting the various convincing proofs which are alledged in favour of chriftianity as well as of a future ftate. I am now fully determined to follow the fame rule in my new principles which I had laid down in regard to my former ones. For my intention was, to think on the approach of death in the following manner : I have examined my idea that every thing ceafes with this life, and

I have

I have found it to be true. Therefore, if I
fhould die, nothing fhall make me think otherwife; and I will die with a confidence, that, in
cafe I fhould be wrong, God is a benevolent
being who will forgive my error. But I fee now
that my former notions of God's mercy are unworthy of the Supreme Being. I have now examined chriftianity with greater exactnefs than I
ever did my old fyftem, and by this examination
I am convinced of its truth. I therefore will
remain firm. Neither my old fyftem, nor new
doubts, fhall henceforth ftagger me."

He then, after fome queftions about the in-
fpired writers, told me, that he now was frequently reading the Bible fince I had given him
one. He faid, " he fhould like to know what
reafons there were to believe the facred books
were really written by thofe authors to whom
they are afcribed."

For this very purpofe I had brought with
me D. Lefs's * book on the truth of the
chriftian religion. I defired him to read it, and
he would find fufficient hiftorical proofs to believe that the books of the New Teftament were

eally

* The Truth of the Chriftian Religion, by D. Lefs,
Profeffor and Doctor of Divinity at Gottingen. Bremen,
1768. 8vo.

really the writings of thofe evangelifts and apoftles to whom they were attributed.

He told me after this, that he frequently prayed to God to enlighten and confirm him in truth. He added, " I am fure God will hear my prayers and blefs my endeavours."

The eleventh Conference. March the 21ſt.

I FOUND him reading D. Lefs's book on. the truth of the chriftian religion, and he faid : " It was fomething remarkable that there were fo very few evidences in the firft century of the authenticity of the books of the New Tefta-ment." To which I replied, that it was owing partly to the books of the New Teftament having been written either about the middle, or towards the end of the firft century, and that for this very reafon but very few copies could be taken; partly that there were but few writers of the firft century that had an opportunity of mentioning any thing concerning the authenticity of the writings of the apoftles.

The Count faid further : " That from the fhort mention made in this book of the chief deiftical writings, he found that the objections againft revelation were but very trifling, and

that

that he was aſhamed of having ſuffered himſelf to be impoſed upon by ſuch inſignificant objeﬅions. He never imagined that chriſtianity was founded upon ſuch ﬅrong arguments, and that they would convince him."—He then ſpoke much in praiſe of thoſe books he had read during his impriſonment; particularly of Gellert's Leﬅures on morality. He wiſhed that thoſe who had been ſeduced by him from virtue might read them. He ſaid, he had in this reſpeﬅ Count Brandt particularly in view, and added; " I hear that he ﬅill is very gay, but I imagine it would make a great impreſſion upon his mind if he was told how my ſentiments are altered. Though he has not been more virtuous than I have, yet he always had a better opinion of religion than I had. Would you be ſo kind as to go to him, and tell him how you find me, and beg him to be now at laﬅ a little more ſerious? Or would you rather write to him ?"

I anſwered, there are difficulties both ways, which may be avoided if you will charge the clergyman who attends Count Brandt with this meſſage. Are you ready and inclined to do this?

" Yes," ſaid he, " bring the Dean Hee to me, I will beg this favour of him in your preſence. I am not aſhamed to confeſs what I am

fo well convinced of. I wifh I had an opportunity to tell it to all my former acquaintance."

Here he told the truth, for hitherto he had
faid nothing to the officers who guarded him;
but now he began to entertain them frequently
with religious converfations. He faid: " that
he had been recommending religion and a virtuous life to an officer, and his anfwer was: He
had nothing to fay againft religion; but to obey
its precepts in regard to fenfual pleafures and
lufts, feemed to him impracticable. He then,
by quoting his own example, fhewed him how
neceffary he himfelf had now found thefe things
to be, and how unhappy they had made him.
He had intreated him to read Gellert often,
who would convince him how ufeful it was
to conquer even our favorite fins."

He added: " What difference is there between
that virtue which chriftianity demands, and that
which the world calls an honeft life? If mere
worldly people, that think in the fame manner
as I have done formerly, fhould judge of my
actions according to their fyftem of morality, I
believe they would think them to be honeft
enough, as I did formerly myfelf."

You

You muft even now, faid I, take great care not to think too well of fome of your actions; to which he replied:

" I know very well that refpecting all my actions, which I thought to arife from good intentions, ambition and voluptuoufnefs had as great a fhare in them as my love towards that which is good. I count them nothing before God and my confcience. When in my former fituation, I fancied to act well and deferving of praife, I thought like the Pharifee in the Gofpel."

From this time, I obferved in the Count, a certain calmnefs and ferenity of mind, which feemed to arife from the hopes that God for Chrift's fake would pardon him. This fituation of his mind had been particularly vifible to his judges in his laft examination. They had not feen him fince the time I had vifited him, and could therefore better obferve the alteration, than I, who had converfed with him fo often during this time. One of them told me, that he had behaved on his examination extremely well, and had appealed once with a vifible joy to that bleffed eternity he hoped to enter into. He had been among them as among his friends, and had talked about his affairs as one who fpeaks about

G

indifferent

indifferent things. His conduct had been very moving to them all.

But fince it appeared to me as if he expected ftill a certain particular fenfation of his being pardoned before God, I endeavoured to fet him to rights in this point. I told him, that with regard to thefe fenfations, the matter was very uncertain. I would not abfolutely deny their exiftence, but I found no Scripture proofs that they were either neceffary or to be expected as certain confequences of repentance and faith. The beft and moft certain conviction of our being pardoned before God was, to be confcious that we repent of our fins fincerely, that we acknowledge Chrift to be our Redeemer, that we perceive our progrefs in godlinefs, and that we moft earneftly endeavour to conform our fentiments and our actions to the will of God. Whoever thinks other fenfations to be neceffary, is in danger of being carried away by enthufiafm.

He then anfwered me, " That he never could bear enthufiafm in religion, and that this was one great reafon that had made him averfe from chriftianity." He faid, " He remembered ftill, that once in that public fchool *, where he had received his inftruction in religion, fome hun-

* The Orphan-houfe at Hall.

dreds

dreds of young people were at once given out to
be illuminated and converted, though he himſelf
was ſure, that ſome of them, with whom he was
nearly acquainted, were very immoral and wicked.
Many ſtrange things had been tranſacted by theſe
converted boys; ſo that he and others that were
not among the number, could not help being
greatly ſcandalized on account of religion."—

I promiſed to bring him Spalding's book on
the value of the inward feelings in Chriſtianity,
that he might inform himſelf more on this point.

The twelfth Conference. March the 24th.

D. HEE, whom I had told of the Count's
deſire to ſpeak to him, came to-day with
me. The Count was not aſhamed to confeſs the
miſtakes of his underſtanding and his heart. He
told the Dean minutely, how he had firſt quitted
virtue and afterwards abandoned religion, and in
what manner he had recovered from his errors.
He expreſſed his fear, that his friend Count
Brandt, through his natural vivacity, might be
hindred from conſidering ſeriouſly on religion and
the condition he was now in. But Count Brandt
having always believed more of religion, than he
himſelf, and ſhewn this even in his converſation, he hoped it would not only be agreeable

to

to him, to hear that he himself was now better informed and convinced, but that it would even make a happy impreffion upon his mind. Formerly he would not hearken to Count Brandt, when he wanted to fpeak to him about religion, but that he now thought it his duty to let him know his prefent fentiments. He looked upon himfelf fo much more obliged to it, fince he was acceffary to his misfortunes.

The Count afterwards continued his converfation thus. " I have been reading the book of D. Lefs, particularly that part which treats on the miracles, reported to have been wrought at the tomb of the Abbé de Paris. I wonder why this affair, that has made fo much noife at Paris, is not by command properly enquired into. I remember myfelf, when I was phyfician at Altona, that I was called upon to examine the ftate of a perfon that was fubject to convulfions, by which means I faw the unexpected and wonderful effects which an extravagant fancy can produce. Such things as the pretended miracles of the Abbé de Paris, fhould not raife any doubts againft the miracles of the Gofpel. But I have other doubts, which appear to me of greater weight. However, I am refolved to think on them no more, for it is enough for me, after a calm examination, to have found the arguments for

chriftianity

chriftianity unexceptionable. Would to God I had time to make myfelf further acquainted with it, and to put it into practice."

He complained that this morning, when he was reading the Gofpel of St. Matthew, many blaf-phemies againft Chrift and the Virgin Mary came into his mind again, which he had formerly read in fome deiftical book. " Now," faid he, " I defpife fuch things, though formerly perhaps they might have raifed fcurrilous thoughts, and hindred my progrefs towards truth."

I brought him Spalding's book on the value of inward feelings in chriftianity *. I told him, that I hoped the reading of it would make religion appear to him in a ftill more amiable light, when he found, how much it was adapted to the nature of the foul, and ftood not in need of incomprehenfibilities, of effects without a caufe, of apparitions, concerning which it remains always matter of doubt, whether they are becoming the wifdom of God. He anfwered:

" This is what I hope likewife. Revelation muft not contradict reafon, fince God has given it to rational beings. The more found and folid

---

* Thoughts on the value of inward feelings in Chrifti-anity. By John Joachim Spalding, Dean of Berlin. Leipfic. 1764. Second edit.

G 3

reafon

reason calls it under examination, the more muft
it profit by it. If thofe things which men have
foifted into religion, were left out in the pulpit
and dogmatical writings, almoft all the weapons
of the deifts would become blunted. I remember very well how much many, perhaps well
intended fermons, which I heard at Halle have
confirmed my unbelief. It was too plain to me,
that thofe things which were told me there could
not be truths revealed by God, though it
was confidently afferted that they were."

The thirteenth Conference. March the 25th.

I COULD ftay but a fhort time with the
Count. The following is the moft remarkable part of our converfation :

" The Count mentioned fome objeftions
againft chriftianity, which he had read in *Boulanger antiquité devoilée*, that fear was the origin
of all religion among the ancients. All calamities
which could befal men, as earthquakes, fires,
inundations, war, &c. they ufed to look upon
as punifhments of their gods, though they arofe
from natural caufes ; and to appeafe the wrath
of their deities they became to think of religion.
He at that time believed Boulanger to have
proved his affertions very clearly from hiftory."

I told

I told him that Boulanger was a writer of no credit, authority, or knowledge, either in antiquity, history or languages. An idiot and a charletan. A man who told untruth, contradicted himself, &c. like another author who wrote the *Evangile du jour*, where he in one place proves, that there was no Moses, because an antient writer Sanchoniaton did not make mention of him, though he lived in the neighbourhood where the history was transacted in which Moses was concerned. And in another place, in order to make Moses a writer of later date, it is asserted that Sanchoniaton lived long before him. To which the Count replied: " That Voltaire was dangerous and captivating merely from wit and humour."

When I was leaving the Count, he expressed his desire to inform in person Count Brandt of his present sentiments about religion, and to tell him of his reformation. He said, " He should do this in the court of justice, if they should happen to be both confronted; but he doubted that this would not be the case, since their confessions agreed together. Therefore, he should beg leave to visit him, and to tell him the same before witnesses. If I were to tell it him myself, it would make a greater impression upon him; and his condition grieves me so much, that I would

willingly

willingly contribute all that is in my power towards his reformation."

The fourteenth Conference. March the 26th.

"I WISH," said he, when I came in, " to have done with thofe affairs I have now upon my hands; for they hinder the regular continuation of our conferences, and keep me from reading. However, I hope to finifh them foon. I know, I want all my time for weightier concerns of my foul. Neverthelefs I have finifhed D. Lefs, and I owe much to this book. It has brought my certainty to a higher degree, on account of the credibility of the miracles, and I can prove now the truth of the chriftian religion from miracles. The book is written with great folidity. The Germans begin to excell in this kind of writing."

I told him, we had another excellent original of this fort, D. Noffelt's Defence of the Chriftian Religion; which he, if time would permit it, might read with great advantage.

We then talked of fome prophefies, which concerned not Chrift in particular, but whole nations, how far they were fulfilled.

The calmnefs and ferenity of the Count's mind encreafed now fo much, that it appeared to me rather a little fufpicious. I therefore thought it

necefſary

neceffary to remind him, not to be carried away by a too quickly produced compofure of mind, and not to forget, fince he had hopes of being pardoned before God, what he had been before his converfion: elfe his former careleffnefs might gain power over him again, and obftruct his endeavours of conforming himfelf to the will of God, which might caufe him a great deal of uneafinefs towards the latter days of his life.

" I affure you," was his anfwer, " that I have not for one moment judged myfelf indulgently, and that hitherto I have not ceafed to repent of my former life ferioufly. I am rather convinced, that even in eternity, happy as it might turn out for me, I fhall remember my fins with horror and deteftation."

On another occafion, he afked, what might be the reafon that phyficians were fo eafily prejudiced againft religion?

I know, faid I, that the religion of phyficians is commonly looked upon as fufpicious; but I think without reafon. You yourfelf muft know many great phyficians that are, without contradiction, profeffed chriftians. Boerhaave, Stahl, Junker, Hofmann, Werlhof, were all chriftians. You are acquainted with Mead's writings in favour of religion. Haller has but lately pub-

lifhed

lifhed a book in behalf of chriftianity, which I fhould give you to read if it was to be had here already. Our Berger, what a profeffed, pious confeffor of religion is he !

" Zimmerman * likewife, added he, is a chriftian. And you muft, upon the whole, not think that I brought this thought upon the carpet as a thing of any real confequence. It is of as little fignification as the opinion I have heard maintained, that Michaelis and Semler were deifts."

If they really were fuch, replied I, they hardly would give themfelves fo much trouble in promoting chriftianity as they really do. This no doubt is an accufation of intolerant chriftians, which is fufficiently refuted by the fervice which thefe men are of to religion.

The fifteenth Conference. March the 27th.

THE Count having fhewed a defire to know fomething more about prophecies, and their being fulfilled, I brought him, for this

* D. Zimmerman is phyfician in ordinary to his Britannic Majefty at Hanover. Some of his writings are lately tranflated into Englifh, particularly his *Effay on National Pride,* and his *Treatife on the Dyfentery.*

purpofe,

purpofe, Newton's Differtations on Prophecies. Among many things he faid:

" I find now of how great importance that moral rule is, to avoid the firft fin. If we do not do this, but allow ourfelves to delight in thinking of irregular defires, without oppofing the firft emotion of them, it is frequently afterwards no more in our power to act well and virtuous. I know this by my own experience. It feemed to me by far too fevere, when Chrift fays, Whofoever looketh on a woman to luft after her, has committed adultery with her already in his heart. The looking on a woman, thought I, even with a defire to luft after her, can be no crime if it goes no further. But the ruminating upon means how to fatisfy our defires, follow in courfe. Whenever I faw means to get my ends, I fancied it very hard if I fhould not make ufe of them. I did ufe them, I fatisfied my luft, and committed a whole feries of fins, which I might have efcaped, if I had avoided the firft fin, the taking delight in the wicked defire, and ftudioufly entertaining it. I then endeavoured to apologize for my crimes. I cannot help it, faid I, that my natural difpofition and temper is fo much for voluptuoufnefs ; it therefore cannot be imputed to me as a crime if I live according to this my difpofition. I was confirmed in this by that

over-

overbearing feverity of thofe who taught me morals in my youth. They never told me that
Chrift did not forbid innocent things, and that
his morals did not deny us harmlefs joys. Every
thing I had an inclination for, was told me to be
fin, without diftinction. To wear ruffles, to
powder the hair, was declared to be as equally
impious as other extravagancies which were
openly finful. I now concluded, that fince it was
impoffible that the firft mentioned things could
be fins, and I found they could not be well
avoided in the world, it perhaps might be the
fame cafe with the others ; they might alfo be
innocent things, and not to be avoided. I know
I was in the wrong; but I was young, my paffions raged, and my leaders fhould have had more
underftanding."

He added : " In the fame manner much harm
is done by thofe teachers of chriftianity who require always a blind obedience, and do not lay
proofs before their hearers of that authority upon
which they fhall build their belief in adopting
thefe truths.—He faid it was neceffary that a
teacher fhould prove the Bible to be a divine revelation : and that whoever would take only
proper time, and was not againft the trouble of
meditating, could never examine chriftianity
without being convinced of its truth. Every
thing

thing is naturally and well connected, and recommends itself to a mind given to reflexion. I never found in deiftical writings a fyftem fo well connected ; and, upon the whole, I am inclined to believe that there is no fuch thing as a regular fyftem of infidelity."

He continued : " No objection can be made to chriftianity, becaufe it promifes rewards to its true profeffors. Love of God, without any relation to ourfelves, is but a mere idea. I am fenfible that I could not continue for a long while to love a friend, who fhewed himfelf always cold towards me. And the Supreme Being cannot be difpleafed with a love, that minds at the fame time our own intereft : for God can reap no advantage from our inclination towards him, but only we ourfelves. And why fhould we not look out for rewards and accept of them, when God himfelf has offered and promifed them ?"

" My great delight in fenfual pleafures perfuaded me always, that as there was nothing of this kind among the joys of heaven, they would have no charms for me."

The sixteenth Conference.　March the 28th.

" I HAVE now finished," said the Count,
" the Acts of the Apostles, and by this
means am informed of the wonderful foundation
of the church of Christ.　It is very visible that
a higher hand promoted this work.　For other-
wise, how could all this have been done in so short
a time, by such persons as the apostles were, and
in spite of such an opposition from all sides ? One
thing rather raised my surprize. I found that Paul
and Peter once did not quite agree.　But when
on the other side I perceived how much they
agreed in the chief point of Christ's resurrection,
of repentance and faith, this matter no longer
puzzled me.　They were men, and therefore
might be mistaken in their private opinions."

" Now and then," said he, " I cannot help
thinking on my situation before my fall.　This
morning I asked myself, whether it would not
have been better for me, if I could have kept
myself in my high station, and enjoyed my usual
pleasures ? But when I had been considering for
a few minutes, I found that I now am by far
more happy than I was in my greatest outward
prosperity.

profperity. I have frequently told my friend Count Brandt that I was by no means happy, when he believed me in many refpects better off than himfelf. You cannot think what an infinite number of things always took up my time. Whatever happened abroad made me uneafy. I was obliged to think of means for my own fafety, and to force myfelf to conceal my uneafinefs both from myfelf and others. The day I fpent in difagreeable occupations and tedious diffipations, and part of the night in reading ftate papers, and in writing. Was it poffible for me to be happy in fuch a fituation? Now I am more ferene and more eafy. I occupy myfelf with religion, which interefts me much, and which is my only comfort. I have an hopeful profpect in eternity, and my death does not difquiet me much, and not very often. How I may be affected at a more trying crifis, I do not know, but I am convinced of my being now happy and compofed, and that I am not defirous of returning into my former fituation."

The feventeenth Conference. March the 30th.

" THE more, faid the Count, I learn chriftianity from Scripture, the more I grow convinced, how unjuft thofe objections are which

it

it is charged with. I find, for inftance, that all
which Voltaire fays of the intolerance of the chriftians, and of bloodfhedding caufed by chriftianity, is a very unjuft charge laid upon religion.
It is eafily to be feen, that thofe cruelties, faid
to be caufed by religion, if properly confidered,
were the production of human paffions, felfifh-
nefs and ambition, and that religion ferved in
fuch cafes only for a cloak. To be convinced
of this, one may read only the hiftory of the cruel
tranfactions of the Spaniards in America."

Having finifhed reading Newton on Prophecies,
he made fome remarks upon this argument in favour of the truth of the chriftian religion, and then
concluded : " My affairs of this world are now
finifhed, a few conferences with my defenfor, and
a few letters, which I intend to write, excepted."

I then told him, that we now could regularly
carry on our conferences, and faid, Let us now
confcientioufly employ the reft of our time in
promoting the great bufinefs of your falvation.
He replied :

" This certainly I fhall do with all poffible
earneftnefs. Thank God! I am fully convinced
of the truth of the chriftian religion, and I feel
its power in quieting my confcience and reforming

ing my fentiments. I hope God will forgive me thofe doubts which perhaps might ftart in my mind, and thofe flight emotions of my former paffions by which I was ruled, and which even now fometimes will difturb me. I find no pleafure in them, and endeavour to fupprefs them immediately. I am ready to convince you by any fact you may demand of me to fhow how ready I am to facrifice my former affections. Never fhould I have done fo before I was enlightened by religion. I do not know whether this is fufficient reafon for you to be fatisfied with me. Try me in what manner you fhall think proper: and if you are fatisfied with me, do not mind if others fhould judge otherwife, according to their opinon, and fay you had attempted to bring me over by reafoning. I acknowledge 't with gratitude before God, that you took this method. In no other manner you would have prevailed upon me. I fhould have oppofed with obftinacy. Perhaps fome impreffion might have been made upon me, but a folid and lafting conviction never would have been brought about. Befides, God cannot be difpleafed, fince religion is fo reafonable, that men are gained over by reafon. Chrift himfelf acted fo, and Paul accommodated himfelf at Athens, and before Felix and Agrippa, to the

way

way of thinking of thofe he had to deal with. I hope the manner, in which I came to alter my fentiments in regard to religion and virtue, will raife the attention of thofe that think as I formerly did. The deifts will never truft the converfion of their brethren, which is brought about in the latter days of their life. They fay, they are taken by furprize through the declamation of the clergyman ; they have loft their reafon ; they are ftupid or frantic by the violence of their illnefs; the fear of death made them ignorant of what they did.——But now fince I came to learn chriftianity, in the manner I did, nobody fhall fay fo. I have examined the chriftian religion during a good ftate of health, and with all the reafon I am mafter of. I tried every argument, I felt no fear, I have taken my own time, and I have not been in hafte. The chief bufinefs which I, for the fake of my own mind's eafe, have ftill to tranfact is, to fearch whether I find thofe figns within me, which are required, if upon a good foundation, I believe myfelf to be pardoned before God."

I gave him a letter of his pious mother, which he took with an air of tendernefs and tranquillity. " He faid, he fhould read it, when alone."——

He

(99)

He added: " I never felt my love to my
parents fo great, as now. I never was fo fully
convinced of their good intentions towards me.
And my good mother! (here a flood of tears
broke forth) She always has loved me with a
kind of preference."

The following is the letter.

Rendfburg, *March* the 17th; 1772.

" Inftead of entertaining you with our mutual
grief and pain, I rather find myfelf under a
neceffity to acquaint you, with thofe prevalent
feelings of my heart, on account of that condition you are in at prefent. Many days and
years the fubject of my prayers to God has been;
that he might fave your immortal foul from
everlafting ruin. I have therefore now facrificed
my defires, which made me, as a mother, wifh
for the happinefs of my children, not only of
their fouls, but likewife of their body. If the
mercy of God cannot otherwife reach the welfare
of your foul, but by means that are hard and
painful to the outward man, I have fubmitted
with an humble and compofed mind, to the
moft holy and moft perfect will of the Lord who
had mercy upon us from everlafting. But never

H 2   could

could I expect that doleful situation you are in now. My maternal heart is thereby crushed to pieces, and as it were immured alive. God is my refuge. My sole comfort under so hard sufferings, will be the salvation of your soul. I shall praise the Almighty with tears of joy, when I hear he, as the friend of sinful men, has still thoughts of peace over you, and that he with thorns has shut up the way which could lead you to everlasting ruin. I do not doubt but the Spirit of God has convinced your mind already, that your Redeemer would not have you lost for ever, since you are his property. Give but farther attention to that work of grace which the Holy Spirit is doing within your soul, for the sake of your conviction. He will reveal to you more, than the tongues of men can make you acquainted with. Think you have to do with nobody, but God and yourself, and remove therefore all your thoughts from things of this world. If the Spirit of God shall have only first glorified Christ within you; if you have been brought so far as to apply to yourself his fully sufficient redemption; you then will count all things but loss for the excellency of the knowledge of Christ Jesus your Lord : you then will count it but dung, that you may win Christ. Your eternal and immortal mind will enjoy al-

ready

ready here more eafe, comfort, and joy, than ever the world, with all its fplendor and pleafure, can afford us. It has pleafed God to convince my foul of this from my youth. There is no happier ftate in the world than to be a true chriftian, both in good and evil days. How much would it have pleafed me, if all my children had likewife let this bleffed conviction be produced within them by the Spirit of God from their youth. But I have found, that this is only a work of God, and not of men. Now, my dear fon, what may have been not properly conducted or neglected by men, let us be truly forry for, and beg God's forgivenefs. But do not defpair of God's mercy, which he has fo clearly revealed in Chrift our Redeemer. Let us not leffen God's intentions, but give a faithful affent to thofe true affertions of Scripture : " God fo loved the world, that he gave his only begotten Son, that whofoever believeth in him, fhould not perifh, but have everlafting life." But all thefe doctrines are fuch, that mere human reafon can neither clear them up fufficiently nor convince us thereof. You muft beg for the affiftance of the Holy Ghoft : for it is he that reveals unto us by his word, Chrift and the great work of his redemption, in a falutary manner. If you

 will

will only set about an examination of the chief
doctrines of our holy religion, with candid and
sincere intentions, and earnest prayer to God for
the enlightening of your understanding, you will
find breaking forth a light in your soul, which
is more than mere natural, and which will serve
you for better insight, and greater confirmation
of these doctrines. I write this after the small
share of knowledge, which the grace of God has
granted me. My faith has, notwithstanding all
the literal knowledge of the revealed truth, been
obliged to work through the most specious objections. But praised be the Lord and his Spirit, who
has strengthened my faith by his word, and by my
own inward experience of its truth, that even the
gates of hell shall not prevail against it, as long
as I keep close to the Omnipotent God, and rid
not myself of him. And this is my anchor in
these my highest sufferings, else the waves of
my distresses would soon set adrift the vessel of
my faith. I wish and beg to God, that he may
grant you this support of your faith. Jesus
Christ is, and remains for ever, the true corner-
stone, upon which the structure of our salvation is
to be begun and to be finished. From your
infancy you shewed a character of mind that was
sincere and without disguise. Let this natural

good

good difposition of yours be fanctified by the Holy Spirit, that you may turn to your God with all fincerity. For God profpers the honeft. Bleffed is the man in whofe fpirit there is no guile. Learn how deeply you are corrupted, and come then as a curfed finner to him who was made a curfe for us. Your father and I will both cry to God and implore his mercy for you. I remain your heartily afflicted mother," &c.

D. Hee came to day again to fee the Count, and to tell him, that Count Brandt greatly rejoiced to hear of his converfion. That he found his only comfort in religion, that he never loft all fenfe of it, and that he from his heart forgave him all that he had done to draw him into his misfortunes. Count Struenfee gave his anfwer very affectingly, and D. Hee took his leave.

The eighteenth Conference. March the 31ft.

MY readers will remember that the Count had already adopted the doctrine of Chrift's redemption, and was therefore a chri-

ftian.

ſtian. He was now ready to acknowledge the other myſteries of religion, which are connected with this doctrine, to be divine. I thought it . neverthelefs neceffary to ſhew him how reaſonable and uſeful they were, that by this his belief might be the better grounded, and that no doubts on account of thoſe myſteries might make him uneaſy. I made therefore firſt the following general obſervations on the ſubject.

If it has pleaſed God, ſaid I, to reveal himſelf to men through Chriſt, his intention was, either to reſtore natural religion among men, which was nearly loſt, and to lay before men, with the higheſt authority, thoſe truths, which were difperfed in thouſands of human writings ; or to reveal them doctrines, which were unknown to mere reaſon, though very neceffary to be known for the happineſs of men. Perhaps God had both theſe intentions.

The firſt of them was certainly very beneficent towards mankind, and particularly worthy of God. The knowledge of natural religion was only to be met with among the Jews, and perhaps a few heathen philoſophers. The end of revelation therefore was to reſtore this ſalutary knowledge, and to adapt it to the capacity of

all

all men. But this was not the whole of the intention; for if Jesus was to teach only natural religion, the preparations, which God made to procure credit for his messenger among men, seem to be too great. The doctrines which Christ preached in this respect, were of such a nature, that mere human reason, as soon as it got acquainted with them, must find them clear and true. Therefore if this had been all, it was unnecessary to confirm the doctrine by means of so many miracles, particularly Christ's resurrection, and the inspiration of his Apostles.

It appears from this, that it was the intention of God, that Christ should reveal unto us doctrines which were unknown to reason, at the same time that he was to teach us natural religion: and since he has done both, it is a proof that both was the intention of his coming. Miracles became now necessary to serve him for credentials of being a messenger of God, and to convince men that those new revealed doctrines which Christ preached, and were above human reason, came from God. You see from this, that a religion, whose author performed miracles, must, according to its intention, contain mysteries.

Besides,

Besides, the incomprehensible doctrines of the christian religion are of such a nature, that they inform us more fully of God and his will, and how a sinful man can be saved. In both respects, it teaches us more than reason does. For instance, reason tells us the unity of God, and revelation adds, that Three Persons are in one Deity. Reason looks out in vain for a sufficient means of reconciliation with God; revelation teaches wherein this means consists. Is it therefore to be wondered at, that this revelation, when it speaks of the infinite and incomprehensible God and his decrees which were unknown to reason, should open unto us such prospects which our eyes cannot fully discern, or which is the same, that it should teach mysteries, and require our faith to believe them? Whoever therefore declines adopting the christian religion, shews himself unacquainted with its intention and its objects. He does not do that justice to religion, which he does to other sciences. For though they contain more mysteries than religion ever did, he nevertheless does not object to them. You yourself, said I, have met with thousands of incomprehensibilities in physic and chemistry, but I suppose you never thought them for this reason altogether dreams and deception. He owned it was true.

I con-

I continued: If God was to reveal unto us myſteries unknown to reaſon, and which concerned himſelf and his will, he muſt do this by ſigns which we could underſtand, and theſe muſt be words. But in the language of men there were no words which could exactly convey that idea God was to communicate to us; for we cannot have words in any language to expreſs an idea we know nothing of. God was therefore to make uſe of ſuch words as conveyed that idea, which he wanted to reveal unto us, as nearly as poſſible; but neverthelefs theſe words muſt always remain imperfect. He cannot apply them in their full ſignification, and with all the ideas annexed to them, to thoſe myſteries, which God has made known to us. They are to be taken only in their primitive and univerſal ſignification, and every thing imperfect is to be ſeparated from them.

I explained this to the Count by ſome examples, which he thought cleared up the matter very much. I ſaid: There are ſome ideas annexed to that relation which ſubfiſts between father and ſon. The father muſt have been before the ſon; he muſt have attained a certain age before he begot the ſon; he muſt have been connected with a perſon of the other ſex. Now if any body was

to

to apply these ideas to the scripture expreſſion, Chriſt is the ſon of God, he would not only miſtake the matter, but even find many contradictions. Suppoſe an inhabitant of Iceland was to explain to an Indian the freezing up of the ſea, he would find no word in the language of an Indian to expreſs this phenomenon. Nevertheleſs he is to ſpeak to the Indian in his own language; he therefore is obliged to make uſe of improper words and images. He could, for inſtance, ſay, In my country the ſea, by the influence of the air, changes, at certain ſeaſons, into ſtone. Now the Indian is right if he thinks, that the ſea in Iceland is ſometimes as hard and ſolid as ſtone; but he is in great danger to repreſent the matter to himſelf quite falſly, if he was to apply the reſt of the properties of a ſtone and its uſe to the ideas of ice: If he ſhould think that houſes were built of ice, and ſerved like ſome ſtones for fuel to cook victuals with.

I now deſired the Count to keep theſe general obſervations concerning the myſteries of religion always before his eyes, ſince I was about propoſing them to him ſingly, to explain their ſcriptural ſenſe, to ſhew that they did not contradict reaſon, and that they were beneficial to mankind.

The

The firſt myſtery connected with the doctrine of redemption is this : Chriſt is the ſon of God. The chief paſſages of Scripture in which this doctrine is told, are, Matth. iii. 17. Mark ix. 7. John iii. 16. This laſt paſſage, where Chriſt emphatically is called the only begotten ſon, ſhews that he is the ſon of God in a far more eminent ſenſe than men, and particularly the pious, who are called children of God.

Now if God calls Chriſt his ſon, what ſhall we think by this ? Chriſt has his eſſence of God, like as a ſon of his father, yet not in the manner that this expreſſion conveys to us, which carries imperfections with it, but in an eminent manner which we cannot explain. Chriſt has the ſame eſſence which the father has, and is therefore perfectly equal with him, Hebr. i. 3. Chriſt the firſt born and only begotten ſon of God is entitled to every perfection of the father, he is united with him in perfect love, as an only ſon is with his father. You ſee from this that the father has repreſented to us that relation which ſubſiſts between him and Chriſt under the image of a father and a ſon, becauſe in the whole human nature no picture is to be found which expreſſes the moſt intimate union more exactly and more perfectly than this.—Do you find now in his repreſentation any thing contradicting ?

"No,

" No, said the Count, here is no contradiction ; the whole myftery lies in the inexplicable manner, by which Chrift has his effence from God the father."

I added : Reafon, therefore, cannot pretend to object any thing to this propofition ; Chrift is the fon of God ; it rather is under an obligation to believe it without contradiction, out of reverence for the teftimony and authority of him who has revealed it unto us.

I now made the remark, that all the myfteries of the chriftian religion are beneficial to mankind, and that it was to our own real advantage to believe them. In this refpect it is very beneficial to us that Chrift is the fon of God. Hence the fon of God is our friend, our benefactor, our Saviour, our interceffor. Is there any thing good which he has promifed us, that he fhould not have it in his power to give it ? Every thing good, both in heaven and upon earth, is his as well as his father's. God will certainly hear his only begotten fon when he intercedes for us. Are we to doubt that he that fpared not his own fon, but delivered him up for us all, fhall not with him alfo freely give us all things ?

Dear

Dear friend, this son of God is your Redeemer. You acknowledge him to be such. Judge now what grace and mercy you may expect of him, if you firmly and confidently trust in his redemption; if you spare no pains to think and act, during the remainder of your life, like him, God, I trust, will not punish you in eternity, but be reconciled unto you through his own son. He will not deny you life everlasting when Christ powerfully intercedes for you. Praised be God, who has enabled you to entertain such a glorious hope, as no power, no splendour, no lust of this world, and not your own reason itself could procure you. May he preserve you in this hope until your death, for Christ's sake !

The Count was very much moved, and promised to read what I had written on the subject of to-day, and which I left him for his further perusal. He had likewise those sheets before him which I had given him upon former subjects to read them over again, to see how all these doctrines stood connected. He said :

" He remembered that we had agreed once, that mere reason could not have found out the doctrine of redemption ; but he found that many heathen nations had attempted to reconcile the Deity, by means of sacrifices."

I answered :

I anfwered : Confcience teaches man to reconcile God for fins committed ; but that facrifices
were thought to ferve for this purpofe, was perhaps founded in the Jewifh difpenfation. Even
mere reafon might have invented facrifices, becaufe they were a proof that we rather would
part with our property than entertain the
thought of being under God's difpleafure. But
that God would give his own fon for a facrifice,
was the manner of reconciliation which we agreed
that reafon itfelf could never have found out.
After this the Count faid :

" One of my former objections comes into
my mind again, which is : Why God could
chufe fo defpicable a people as the Jews were,
for his peculiar one ?"

When I had anfwered, that it might be, becaufe they were defcendants of Abraham the
friend of God, of whom they had received
the true natural religion, and that they formerly
were not fo defpicable as they now are thought
to be, he added :

" It is true, we cannot prove from their being
fo defpicable at prefent, that they have been
always fo. Befides, the defpicablenefs of a nation,

tion, is entirely a relative notion. An Englifh-man defpifes a Frenchman, and a Frenchman thinks his nation the moft refpectable one under the fun."

The nineteenth Conference. April the 1ft.

THE Count being told that fince he be-lieved the doctrine of redemption, he could not but believe the other myfteries, be-caufe they were founded upon the fame authori-ty; he anfwered:

" I fhall make no difficulties about that; if the one be true, the other muft be fo likewife. You have hitherto fatisfied my reafon, and I do not doubt but you will be able to do it further."

I continued: If Chrift is the only begotten Son of God, and has of God his divine Effence, he muft be the true God. The New Teftament and Chrift himfelf teaches this. It appears likewife from John v. 18. that the Jews under-ftood him very well, for they fought the more to kill him, not only becaufe he had broken the Sabbath, but faid, that God was his father, making himfelf equal with God. Chrift con-

firmed

firmed what he had faid, by what follows, particularly ver. 21, 22, 23. Let us mind the following three reafons: "The Son quickeneth
whom he will; all judgment is committed unto
the Son; all men fhould honour the Son, even
as they honour the Father."

St. Paul treats likewife, Heb. i. of the
divinity of Chrift. He calls him the " Son of
God, by whom the worlds are made; The
brightnefs of God's glory, and the exprefs image
of his perfon." He applies an expreffion of
Pfal. xlv. 7. where God is addreffed, to Chrift,
and calls him abfolutely God.

When I had read and explained to the Count,
the two paffages of John v. and Heb. i. he
faid: " It is undeniable, that it was the intention
of Jefus and of Paul to tell the Jews that the
Son is God."

Having more fully propofed and proved this
doctrine of Chrift's Divinity, the Count, at the
conclufion of the whole, faid:

" I cannot defcribe to you, how much my
reafon is fatisfied on account of thefe myfteries
of religion. The more we think upon them,
the

the more of divine wifdom we difcover in them. We muft only avoid afking every where: Why?—We muft reft fatisfied with the authority of their author. Even in human fciences this modefty is requifite: elfe we never fhould come to any certainty. Moft common things may employ our refearches for all our life time, before we difcover the firft caufe. Every *why?* would draw innumerable queftions of the fame nature after it, though our reafon is not calculated to go *in infinitum.*"

The Count had now finifhed the hiftory of Chrift's fufferings, and had found the miracles that happened at the death of Chrift very remarkable. He afked:

" If any other hiftorians, befides the Evangelifts, made any mention of them?"

He was told that Phlegon, Tertullian and Lucian, made mention of this famous eclipfe. Upon this the Count faid:

" He had fpoken yefterday with fomebody, who would not allow thefe events to be real miracles, becaufe they could be fully accounted for by mere natural caufes; but that he had told him, it was neverthelefs remarkable,

that

that thefe events fhould have happened at the time when Chrift died, and even at the hour of his death. It feemed as if God, even by this very circumftance, would raife people's attention to the death of Jefus."

I told him, he might have added, that this eclipfe happened on the day before Eafter, when, at the time of the full moon, this event could not take place in the natural way.

The father of the Count had defired me in a letter, which I had lately received, to affure his fon of the continuation of his love and inter-ceffion before God. I communicated to him the letter. He would fain have anfwered fome-thing, but his grief of heart prevented it. When I left him half an hour after: " He begged me with tears in his eyes, to write to his parents, and to tell them that he certainly hoped to afford them the only comfort they wifhed for, which was, to find them again before the throne of God, amongft thofe that have received mercy."

3

The twentieth Conference. April the 3d.

THE chief subject of this Conference was the doctrine of the Trinity, as it is taught in the christian church. This doctrine being stated to him in the most simple manner, he said :

" It appeared to him so as to excite his veneration. But as he was now a convinced christian, as to the theoretical parts of Christ's religion, he wished only to be the same, as to the practical parts of it."

I gave him joy of having now adopted the religion of Jesus with all his heart. If you now lose your life, you will find infinite compensation in eternity.—He answered :

" Certainly I shall lose nothing. The loss would have been irreparable, if I had remained in my former situation. For in all probability I should never have become a christian. But I know now for certain, that if it was possible for me to live any longer in this world, I should never quit religion again. I have been

I 3

often-

oftentimes obftinate in my opinions, and here I fhould be fo for good reafons."

He being told in what manner he might fhew and convince himfelf of being a practical chriftian ; he faid :

"I am ready to do any thing demanded in this refpect.   It gives me pleafure to find myfelf willing for this.   I look upon it as a good fign. Formerly I fhould not have been fo.   I would not have facrificed my vicious inclinations.   I fhall confider in what manner I may give you and myfelf convincing proofs of the fincerity of my prefent fentiments.   You frequently have dropt a hint, as if you thought I had ftill too great an opinion of my adminiftration of public affairs.   I have taken my own time to go into the detail of it; I have fearched the very fprings, and I will not conceal before you the refult of my enquiries.   Believe me then, that I had no intention of doing mifchief.   Voluptuoufnefs and vanity were the fprings of all that I did.   The great opinion I had of my abilities, and which was fupported by others, made me refolve, at my firft coming into Denmark, to act a great part.   I cannot fay I ever imagined it would be fuch as I have fince acted.   But

you

you know, opportunities and circumftances lead us fometimes farther than we thought of in the beginning. One ftep follows the other. Even from this you may conclude, that I abfolutely muft find the whole chain of my enterprizes reproachful before God and my own confcience. —But at the fame time, I am confcious, that I was no enemy to what the great world called virtue and honefty. I do not tell you this in my own praife. I know this is not owing to my endeavours, but rather a confequence of my natural way of thinking, and every man has a certain general love of virtue. That I miffed my intention, was my own fault. I was looking out for what is good, but I did not find it, for I took not reafon and religion, but paffion for my guide."

He had now finifhed Spalding's book on the value of the inward feelings of chriftianity. He returned me thanks for having it given to him, and added:

" My ideas of that reformation in man, which is to be brought about by converfion, are greatly rectified by this book. I own with joy, I find chriftianity more amiable the more I get acquainted with it. I never knew it before.

I 4

I be-

I believed it contradicted reason and the nature of man, whose religion it was designed to be. I thought it an artfully contrived and ambiguous doctrine, full of incomprehensibilities. Whenever I formerly thought on religion in some serious moments, I had always an idea in my mind how it ought to be, which was, it should be simple and accommodated to the abilities of men in every condition. I now find christianity to be exactly so; it answers entirely that idea which I had formed of true religion. Had I but formerly known it was such, I should not have delayed turning christian till this time of my imprisonment. But I had the misfortune to be prejudiced against religion, first through my own passions, but afterwards likewise through so many human inventions, foisted into it, of which I could see plainly that they had no foundation, though they were stiled essential parts of christianity. I was offended when God was always represented to me as an angry jealous Judge, who is much pleased when he has an opportunity of shewing his revenge, though I knew he was love itself; and am now convinced, that though he must punish, yet he takes no kind of delight in it, and is rather for pardoning. From my infancy, I have known but few christians that had not scanda-
lized

lized me by their enthufiafm, and wickednefs, which they wanted to hide under the cloak of piety. I knew indeed that not all chriftians were fuch, or talked fuch an affected language; but I was too volatile to enquire of better chriftians after the true fpirit of religion. Frequently I heard fermons in my youth, but they made no impreffion upon me. That without Chrift there was no falvation, was the only truth which ferved for a fubject in all fermons, and this was repeated over and over again in fynonimous expreffions. But it was never fet in its true light, and never properly proved. I faw people cry at church, but after their tears were dried up, I found them in their actions not in the leaft better, but rather allowing them-felves in every tranfgreffion, upon the pri-vilege of being faithful believers. Laftly, I could not comprehend thofe inward feelings which many chriftians pretend to have. It ap-peared to me unnatural and miraculous. Never-thelefs, it has made me uneafy during our ac-quaintance, that I have found nothing of thefe inward feelings: and I believe you have ob-ferved my uneafinefs. I found my real forrow for my fins not adequate to thofe expreffions, which I had heard frequently in my youth, and which had terrified me fo much. I endeavour-

ed

ed to heighten my grief to such a degree: but I saw on the other side, that this forcing myself, by means of imagination, was not that grief I sought for, or what might have pleased God. Spalding's book has satisfied me on this account. I am now sure that the chief point is a confidence in God through Christ, and a true reformation of mind from what is bad to what is good. I myself can find out and be sensible, whether I have this confidence, and I myself am able to judge, whether such a reformation has taken place within my mind.

The twenty-first Conference. April the 4th.

I Repeated to the Count all we had done together hitherto, and surveyed with him afresh the whole way that brought him to where he now was. After which he said:

" That his present ease of mind was quite a different thing, from what he believed he had formerly. Now he found himself really composed, whereas he formerly only forced himself to appear

to

to be fo. Perhaps he might have been able to die with an outfide appearance of firmnefs, but he believed he fhould have found himfelf quite different, from what he hoped to find now in the hour of death."

The formal impeachment of the Count was to come on in a few days, and he was fummoned to appear in perfon to hear it, and to produce what he might have to fay in his defence.

This he told me, and afked my advice, whether he fhould let his affairs have their own way, or, whether he fhould make the beft defence he could?

I told him, chriftianity never forbad him to ufe all lawful means to fave himfelf.

" Among the crimes," faid he, " that will be laid to my charge, there is one incapable of any apology or mitigation. I fee therefore that the probability of faving my life is by far inferior to that of fuffering death. And befides, I fee nothing pleafing before me, even if I fhould fave my life. Imprifonment for life would be unfupportable to me. However, I cannot deny

that

that I fhiver when I think on the hour of death under fuch circumftances! Confider, if you pleafe, what you would advife me to."

I do not fee any hopes for you, faid I. Government has ordered you a council. He knows the laws better than I do, and therefore can tell you beft what you have to hope, and what not. Your judges are confcientious men, and well verfed in the law.

" I am convinced of that, faid he ; they treated me like honeft people."

Being advifed not to flatter himfelf with vain hopes of faving his life, he gave me his hand, and promifed that he would guard againft it.

" I believe, faid he, God will not be difpleafed, that I feel the inftinct of preferving my life, which he himfelf has implanted. I hope, at the fame time, that if I am to die, even then I fhall be fupported by a profpect (at leaft) of not being worfe off in eternity than I am now.—And do you think I fhould do wrong, if I, at my approaching painful and ignominious death, call to my affift-ance all the natural and even acquired fortitude which I am poffeffed of ?"

I told

I told him it would not be wrong if he did, but without any views of vanity. I hoped, however, religion would afford a much better and a much furer comfort, and prove a fupport adequate to his fufferings.

He read at prefent the Epiftles of Paul to the Corinthians; and faid, he obferved in St. Paul a great genius, much wifdom, and true philofophy. He was particularly pleafed with his decifion of the difputed queftion : Whether it was right to eat what was facrificed to the idols ? He faid, it did honour to his prudence.

I now gave him Spalding's fermons to read, which he took with great readinefs, being very partial to the author.

The twenty-fecond Conference. April the 6th.

TO fhew the Count how far his reformation and his intentions of doing good were fincere, and how far his hopes of having received God's mercy were well grounded, I laid the following queftions for felf-examination before him, and took his anfwers down in writing, that I might confider them by myfelf when alone, and tell him afterwards my opinion how far I found them agreeing with the fenfe of the Gofpel.

The

The following are the principal queſtions and his anſwers.

Are you heartily ſorry that you have offended God by thoſe voluptuous thoughts and actions of which you find yourſelf guilty?

" I look upon it as one of my greateſt crimes, and know that it has led me further and further from that truth which I might have found in the knowledge of religion, and I conſider it as the principal ſource of all my crimes and vices."

Do you think on theſe tranſgreſſions with deteſtation, which gave you, according to your former ſentiments, the greateſt pleaſure?

" I think not only with indifference on all thoſe ſenſual pleaſures, but even I hate them, ſince I find how oppoſite and detrimental they are to real happineſs."

Do you believe, that if you had for the future any more opportunities to commit theſe ſins, you would avoid them out of obedience to God?

" I am ſure I ſhould not be able to avoid them for any other reaſon. Therefore, ſince I begin to taſte the happineſs of virtue, and am ſure that I cannot acquire it but by a true fear of
God

God and the defire of acting according to his will, I am determined never to lofe fight of this. I fhall endeavour to rectify all my principles and actions by the efficacious affiftance of thefe means, which I am become acquainted with through the knowledge of God and his revelation."

Are you truly forry becaufe you have offended God by leading on to immorality, and by making unhappy, through your inclination for fenfual pleafures, not only certain particular perfons, but other people likewife?

" I am extremely forry that I have rendered unhappy fome perfons by my principles, inconfideratenefs, and inclination for fenfual pleafures, not only by hindering their temporal welfare, but likewife by corrupting their moral character. At the fame time I repent very much that I have fet fo bad an example, and thereby fpoiled the good morals of others. I reproach myfelf on account of thofe perfons whom I have actually feduced."

Do you deteft thofe tranfgreffions to which your ambition has inftigated you? the falfe principles upon which you founded your ambition, and the unlawful means you have ufed to fatisfy it?

" The

" The firft moral principles, according to which I acted, were againft God's precepts, and were founded upon a fyftem of honour which I myfelf had formed, and where the principal view was always to gratify my own defires and felf-in-tereftednefs. According to my prefent conviction, I cannot but think the whole chain of my actions in regard to honour reproachful, even then when I might juftify or excufe them before the world."

Are you forry that the happinefs of fo many people, befides that of your friends, who fuffer with you now, has been made, a facrifice to your ambition, during the time of your exalted ftation ?

" I own I cannot excufe before God my having thought too flightly of other people's happinefs. I abufed the maxim that a fingle member of fo-ciety might fuffer for the benefit of the whole. God has recommended to us the love of our neighbour as the chief of virtues, which requires that every one fhall promote the temporal welfare of fingle perfons as much as lies in his power, at leaft fhall he not deftroy it. All my political reafons, which then determined me to act fo, will not excufe me or quiet my confcience. And as for the misfortunes of my friends, I feel them

them so much the more, since my natural tenderness on this point disposes me already for it."

Do you repent of that presumption with which
you placed yourself at the helm of administra-
tion, gave laws, and trifled with the happiness
of the nation ?

" I find myself guilty of this in my conscience.
If even I could derive some excuses from the
circumstances I was in, and which drew me in
further than I thought in the beginning; I am
nevertheless always to be blamed, for not making
a stronger opposition, and not taking my motives for doing it from religion, where I might
have found them."

Are you fully determined to profess christianity until your end, and will you ever act according to its precepts ?

" I now glory as much in christianity and in
acknowledging my former errors, as I then
did in treating it with contempt. My resolution,
which is founded upon conviction, gives me the
surest hope that I, in all circumstances, shall keep
to it, and observe its precepts until my end."

Are you conscious that you bear no hatred
against those whom you think your enemies, nor

K

against

againſt thoſe who have promoted your preſent misfortunes ?

" Since my temper is not revengeful, I am leſs inclined to hatred, and I truſt that thoſe perſons who are the cauſe of my misfortunes, have been acting from conviction, and with an intent to promote the intereſt of the king and the kingdom. And if even ſome people ſhould have acted from perſonal enmity, I forgive it very readily."

Are you conſcious that you ſpoke the truth before your judges, and in your converſation with me? Do you likewiſe propoſe to ſpeak truth in what you ſhall ſay to your counſel, in your defence?

" I do not remember to have ſpoken before my judges one untruth wilfully, unleſs, perhaps, for want of memory, ſome miſtake has happened. Still leſs do I know of any thing untrue which I might have ſpoken to you. I intend likewiſe not to ſay any thing in my defence, that ſhould not agree with truth."

Do you find a true deſire to be pardoned by God, through the merits of Chriſt, and do you truſt in God that he will not refuſe it?

" I have

" I have no other hopes but what are founded in God's pardon, and I am convinced, that there are no other means for me to obtain it but the merits of Chrift. I ftrive to qualify myfelf for this through fincere faith in my Redeemer, and by making my thoughts and fentiments conformable to his will. I pray to God to ftrengthen me in this refpect, fince I find within myfelf nothing but incapacity and weaknefs."

Do you look upon this pardon of God as the greateft favour that can be conferred upon you ; greater than even the faving of your temporal life ?

" The faving of my life and all other temporal emoluments appear to me but very fmall in comparifon of everlafting happinefs, which my inward feeling has made me experience already."

Do you acknowledge yourfelf obliged, on account of this pardon, to love God and your Redeemer fincerely, and will you ftrive to increafe this love ?

" The more I grow convinced, the more impreffion the mercy of God and of my Redeemer makes upon me, and increafes my love and gratitude towards him."

K 2

Are

Are you determined to shew this love towards God, by a ready obedience to his will, as long as you shall have time for it?

" Since I hope to be more and more convinced of the love of God towards me, and since I acknowledge that what he has decreed relating to me, is in all respects, particularly in regard to my soul, the most advantageous, I am sure that I shall submit to all his will, without murmuring and without reluctance."

Suppose your death should within a few days, by the interposition of God's government, become unavoidable, would you suffer it humbly and confiding in God, terrifying as the circumstances may be which shall attend it?

" As much as lies in my power, supported by that confidence which I place in God, I shall die with a christianlike resolution.

Are you resolved to derive all your comfort only from religion, and not to call in for assistance a secret ambition, or an affected fortitude?

" I have resigned every thing which may be called ambition, and have been obliged to do it; I am therefore sure that in the last moments of my life I shall not be disturbed by this passion. I rather

I rather ſhall derive all my comforts from religion. Even my former ambition would not
have led me to affectation. Without religion I
ſhould have died as to my outward appearance
juſt as I felt myſelf inwardly. Properly ſpeaking,
I have been obſtinate only in defending my opinions, and in this reſpect I might, perhaps, too
often have been guilty of affectation."

The Count aſſured me, on the cloſe of this
examination, that he in all reſpects had told me
exactly the ſentiments of his heart.—When I was
going to leave him, he begged I would ſtay a
little longer, ſince he had ſomething to communicate to me.

" I have been conſidering, ſaid he, about
what I aſked your advice the other day. I ſee
plainly my life cannot be ſaved; I am likewiſe
eaſy about it, and I hope the wiſh to live longer
will diſturb me no more, though I do not know
how I ſhall be affected when I am very near death.
If the awful moment was but once paſt, I then
ſhall have loſt nothing. If, when I am going to
ſuffer death, I am but capable of thinking, I am
ſure to find compoſure and comfort in religion."

And if you ſhould not be able to remember,
ſaid I, I ſhall put you in mind of it, though I do
not know how much I myſelf ſhall be affected.

K 3

" I wiſh

" I wish only you may not be too much affected, said he, for this would add to my sufferings."

I shall do as much as I can to moderate my
tender feelings, and I believe to be able to do
this, if I can have hopes that you die a christian.

" I have been, said he, very uneasy about
another thing. You know my chief crime.
You know that by confessing it, other persons to whom I lie under great obligations,
are rendered likewise unhappy. I have been
thinking whether it had not been my duty, on
their account, not to have confessed, since gratitude and friendship seemed to demand it. I have
been very uneasy about it. But I took to prayers,
as now my constant practice is, when I am
under anxiety, and considered this whole matter on all sides, directing my heart perpetu-
ally towards God. I found that my denying
would hinder truth from appearing, and from
making its way as it ought. I saw that it would
be still worse to cover one crime with another,
which would fill me with anxiety of conscience,
and make me incapable of receiving God's pardon. And certainly the request would be unjust,
that for the sake of saving others I should sacri-
fice my everlasting salvation. I found, lastly,

that

that if I had denied every thing hitherto, I now should have discovered it to you, and desired you to acquaint my judges with it. By reasoning in this manner, I have been so fortunate as to quiet my mind. I do not care now if people, who have no notion what it is to be anxious about everlasting salvation, should think me to be both a faithless man and a traitor. My confession must be approved of by all true and rational christians. However, the misfortune that has befallen my friends on account of my confession, grieves me more than I am able to express : I can pay them no other damages, but by praying to God to give them the comfort of religion and virtue. This is what I continually am praying for ; and if these prayers are granted, I am sure their loss is sufficiently repaid."

The twenty-third Conference. April the 7th.

THE Count being told that his answers to the questions proposed to him yesterday were such as proved, that he hitherto had fulfilled those conditions, under which God had promised to grant his pardon, he said :

" I thank God that my peace of mind is likewise a proof of my being not rejected by God. I cannot but persuade myself, that although now

in

in my fetters, and near a difgraceful death, I am by far more happy than I was in my former grandeur."

When I had convinced him from Scripture paffages, that my judgment was well grounded, and had comforted him by telling him, that the more he got acquainted with the advantages of his converfion, the more his faith would increafe, and fupply him with infinite comfort againft death, he faid :

" Yes, I hope to experience that my death is but one difficult ftep, and every thing I lofe by it fhall infinitely be repaid to me."

Some exhortation being given, he faid: " That every night he examined himfelf whether he had done or thought any thing that might difpleafe God ; if fo, he prayed for forgivenefs for Chrift's fake, and repeated all his good pur-pofes, together with their motives. I believe likewife, faid he, that I can pray now with more chearfulnefs. Hitherto I found myfelf always unworthy, but I have ventured to pray, trufting to God's mercy."

Being advifed to thank God for all the grace he had fhewn him during the time of his converfion, he anfwered :

" I remember

" I remember with gratitude thofe powerful impreffions made upon me by perufing many of the paffages in thofe books I have been reading; in particular when I was reading the Life of Chrift. I own my inclination to look out for truth and to embrace it, has increafed thereby from time to time."

Juft when I was leaving the Count, he faid: " I am come now to a refolution how I fhall act in regard to my defence. I fee neither my life can be faved, nor my actions be juftified, neverthelefs, I hope to be able to fhew, that fome are not quite fo bad as they appear to be; for you know, to confider our actions in a moral light before God, and in a political one before the world, are two different things. I know how bad mine appear in the former; but it does not follow that a thing fhould be equally as bad when confidered in a political light, as it may be in a moral one. I fhall reft fatisfied to fhew (for more I cannot do) that my political miftakes were the confequences of error, precipitation and paffion, but not of a defign to do mifchief. I think I owe this to truth, and even religion itfelf, as far as my converfion may either promote or hinder its intereft. If, by keeping filence, I had allowed that I had bad intentions (though I do not recollect any

myfelf),

myfelf), it perhaps then could eafily have happened, that my converfion would have been looked
upon as weaknefs and confufion of mind, notwithftanding it is the produce of a ferious and rational
difquifition.   The world might elfe have faid,
that a man could eafily facrifice his former principles of religion, when it was a matter of indifference to him, whether he was thought to be a
profeffed rogue, or only a man who had tranf-
greffed from error in judgment."

The twenty-fourth Conference. April the 9th.

AFTER reciting the happy confequences of
his converfion, I afked the Count if any
one of thofe days of his former grandeur and temporal profperity had ever procured him that true
tranquillity of mind which he now enjoyed in his
prifon and in his fetters ?

" You are in the right, anfwered the Count;
and if nothing elfe had made me unhappy, the
infatiablenefs of my paffions would have done it,
for the moft frequent enjoyments could not fatisfy them."

He fpoke likewife very fenfibly about his approaching death.   " He declared that death itfelf (the terrifying circumftances which his might

be attended with excepted) prefented nothing dreadful to him, fince he knew where it was to conduct him." He declared:

" It fhould not make him uneafy, if there was even any truth in the opinion of thofe who afferted, that the foul, when feparated from the body, fhould be in a ftate of obfcure ideas and fenfations, or in a kind of fleep. For if my foul was not confcious of itfelf, or was only in a place of fecurity and eafe, I fhould lofe nothing by it. Should this fleep laft even a thoufand or ten thoufand years, it would not make me unhappy, for during all this time, I fhould not know of any thing. However, it is by far more agreeable to me to learn from Scripture, that my foul, inftantly after parting from the body, fhall enter, confcious of itfelf, into poffeffion of its happinefs."

Towards the clofe of this converfation, he faid : " Though Scripture tells us but little about the ftate the foul fhall be in during its feparation from the body, yet even this little is matter of great comfort. If God had found it ufeful and neceffary to give us further information, he would have done it. It is fully fufficient to quiet my foul, when I know it will be in the hand of God.—From this you may judge

how

how much it muſt vex me, if now and then this thought returns : ' perhaps there is no eternity !' I examined myſelf to-day very ſtrictly, if perhaps I found a ſecret pleaſure therein, or if I entertained an obſcure notion of its being true : but I profeſs I found neither of them. There is not a ſhadow of probability left of my former ſyſtem, and the ſtrong proofs of the contrary are always before my eyes. Beſides, I am ſo much intereſted in my being at preſent better informed, that I would not part with my conviction upon any account, or act wilfully contrary to it. If by committing any crime, even ſuch as the world did not acknowledge to be ſuch, I could gain the greateſt temporal advantage, I am confident I ſhould not commit it. If I was promiſed for certain, my life ſhould be ſpared, and that I ſhould be reſtored to my former ſituation, under condition that I contradicted the confeſſion I have made of my crimes, and that I confirmed with an oath my new aſſertion, I am ſure I ſhould rather die than contradict truth, and take ſuch an oath. I am convinced I never ſhould think thus, where I was not perſuaded of eternity, and rather wiſhed or thought it to be a vain fancy. But I ſee now how difficult it is to extirpate ſuch falſe ideas, as we were formerly fond of."

The

The Count had read Spalding's fermons, and affured me he was much edified by them. Some of thofe books which had contributed much to enlighten and reform him, he fent to Count Brandt, for whom he fhewed the tendereft care. I gave him this day Doddridge's *treatife on the rife and progrefs of religion in the foul.*

He defired me to write to his parents, and to comfort them by the account I could now give them of him.

The twenty-fifth Conference. April the 11th.

A Converfation which the Count had with a perfon who difliked the reading of the Bible, on account of its ftile, gave occafion to fome remarks on the ftile of the Bible. Among the reft he obferved, that the ralleries of the freethinkers about Chrift and his doctrine, were plain proofs, that they had no intention of acting honeftly. "It is in general impertinent, faid he, to turn a virtuous man into ridicule. The old and unufual expreffions of the Bible cannot be the true reafon, for which they fhould think them deferving ridicule. They do not laugh at other ancient writings, which are written in fuch a ftile. If they, for inftance, were to read the books of Confucius, I am fure they

would

would not hefitate about his ftile, but praife his morals. In the' fame manner, they extoll the fables of Æfop, but the parables and narrations of Chrift will not pleafe them : notwithftanding they are derived from a greater knowledge of nature, and contain more excellent morality. Befides, they are propofed with a more noble and artlefs fimplicity, than any writings of this kind, among ancient or modern authors. There muft be therefore fomething elfe which prejudices them againft Chrift ; and I do not know what elfe it could be, but their heart, which makes them averfe to his precepts."

Some days fince, the Count had obtained leave to have pen and ink ; and he faid, " he would make ufe of it, to draw up the account of his converfion, which he had promifed to leave behind him."

It will be, faid I, a very acceptable legacy to me. Write with reflection, and I hope it will not be ufelefs. It fhall remain an authentic monument of your religion and piety. I therefore leave it entirely to you, to arrange your thoughts and to write them down. I will have no other fhare in it, than to tell

you

you in general terms, how it is to be drawn up
fo as to anfwer its intention. This intention
is partly to efface thofe impreffions your example has made upon the minds of others,
partly to raife the attention of thofe that are of
the fame way of thinking as you formerly were.
It muft therefore appear by this writing, that
your fentiments about religion and virtue are
really altered. At the fame time, you are to
relate how this alteration was produced. I think
this to be neceffary, left any body fhould doubt
its truth. As to your ftile and expreffions, it
muft be fuch, as will not be difpleafing to the
people of the world, and that others may not
entertain any doubt of your having become a
chriftian.

" I fhall endeavour," faid he, " to keep
thefe rules before my eyes. But if you find
any miftake, that I perhaps was not fufficiently
acquainted with fome doctrines, or that fome
paffages may be liable to cenfure, you are always
at liberty to correct them."

No, replied I, not a fingle word fhall I
attempt to alter. It muft be entirely your
own, for fear fome people fhould think it
fpurious.

The

The Count remembered the late Reverend Mr. Alberti of Hamburgh, with whom he was perfonally acquainted, and wifhed to read his fermons, which I fent him.

The twenty-fixth Conference. April the 13th.

" ALberti's fermons," faid the Count, " have much edified me. They have likewife contributed to make me have a greater regard for religion, and at the fame time made me more compofed and happy."

The to-day's converfation turned upon the doctrine of the refurrection of the body. The Count having been made acquainted with the arguments in favour of it, faid :

" He believed the chief objections againft the refurrection of the body, were ftarted after it had been pofitively afferted by. Chrift. From that time, thofe who had a bad confcience, became fearful. They endeavoured to fecure themfelves by fuch objections, againft anxious expectations." He added, after fome other reflexions, " That death was not indifferent to

him,

him, but yet not terrible. Neverthelefs, he could not deny, but that he had great reafon to repent of thofe actions by which he had haftened it; yet, fince this could not be altered, and he was fure that his fins would be forgiven, he had nothing that could attach him to this life, except the natural inftinct of felf-prefervation; and he was ready to leave this world as foon as God pleafed to call him. He did not care what might become of his body after his deceafe, for it was fafe every where under God's care. In the mean time, he would make the beft ufe of his time he could, and endeavour to become every day better and more acceptable to God. For this purpofe, faid he, I read, I pray, I reflect on my former and my prefent fituation, and compare them both; I fpeak to the officers about religion and virtue, but without intruding and without affectation."

The twenty-feventh Conference. April the 14*th.*

FUture judgment, and everlafting rewards and punifhments, were the fubject of this Conference. With regard to eternity and future punifhments, the Count expreffed himfelf in this manner:

L" If

" If even the punishments of a future world, were only to last during the life of a man, it would be very terrifying, and sufficient to keep us from sin. It would be dreadful enough if the punishments consisted in nothing else but the natural consequences of sin, without any further dispensations of God. I thought men might be punished in eternity by those passions to which they were addicted in this world. They leave this world with all their internal appetites, which attend them in all their strength. There is nothing in the other world to satisfy these desires. They consume themselves in insatiable longings, and vain wishes. God need only say to them : You shall remain as you are."

Being told that since his salutary reformation, he joyfully might expect his sentence before God's tribunal, he replied, " That he really waited with joy for it, and trusted in God's mercy." He said, " His objections, which he formerly thought unanswerable, were now quite gone, or at least of so little consequence, that he doubted about the truth of religion no more than about my being with him. He was now so conscientious, that he examined every
thing

thing he did and thought, whether it agreed with
the will of God. And he found himself by
this fo well, fo compofed, fo happy, that he
was fure, he fhould conftantly think and act
in the fame manner."

As the time of his death drew near, I thought
proper to infpire him with ideas of futurity;
for which purpofe I gave him Lavater's Profpects into eternity.

The twenty-eighth Conference. April the 17th.

TO day our converfation turned partly upon
eternity. On occafion of the explanation of feveral paffages of Scripture, that have
a relation to this fubject, the Count admired
the propriety of St. Paul's expreffions, and the
images he made ufe of.

" I find now," faid he, " that I from time
to time get more acquainted with the ftile of the
Apoftles. They write extremely well, now
and then inimitably beautiful, and at the fame
time with fimplicity and clearnefs." He quoted
feveral paffages, particularly from the eighth
chapter to the Romans. He added, " I fhould
 like

like to see other publicans and tent-makers, write in the same manner as the Evangelists and Apostles did."

Being reminded that his uncommon and unexpected calmness and composure of mind, was a consequence of his being certain of God's pardon, he said:

" It is certainly a consequence of my being pardoned for Christ's sake, and of my being conscious that my sentiments are altered; and this accounts for those ill founded ideas of the feelings in christianity. The composed mind which christianity procures, is such a feeling. I have it now myself. They were only mistaken in explaining the reasons thereof. Why should God produce these sensations by miracles, when they are the natural off-spring of a well founded conviction, and a true conversion ?"

Towards the end of the conversation, he declared, " That he thought himself very happy in being so near eternity, though the manner in which he entered into it must be melancholy for him. In the mean time, he would do every thing in his power, to be in a situation in which he might hope to overcome the terrors of death,

and

and to be certain of an happy immortality. He believed, his duty in this point confifted chiefly in having his former life continually before his eyes, that he might keep up a lively fenfe of repentance, and in ftriving to confirm himfelf in his prefent fentiments, to mind them, and to accuftom himfelf more and more to them. This, faid he, is now my whole occupation; it is fo interefting to me, and pleafes me fo well, that nothing is more agreeable to my tafte. A little while ago I ufed, as I told you, to read fometimes *L' hiftoire generale des voyages.* I then thought that I could employ my time better. But not being willing to appear in my own eyes in a hypocritical light, I would not forcibly fupprefs my inclination for this book. This inclination has now left me. I do not like to read, or to meditate on any thing elfe, but what concerns my chief bufinefs, which is a preparation for eternity. Thank God, I am advanced now fo far, that my doubts do not make me any more uneafy. What you told me in the beginning, I find to be true, for no objection prefents itfelf but what I am able to anfwer to my fatis-faction."

" The

" The christian religion," said he on another occasion, " is so engaging, that it certainly must please every one who is properly acquainted with it. We should see the best effects of it among the common people, in reforming the world, if it was properly represented, and made intelligible to the capacity of different sorts of people. They should be made sensible, that in this life they could never be happier than by following the precepts of christianity. Every one then would be convinced, that, supposing even this religion to be a delusion, it must be such an one as contradicts entirely the nature of error and delusion, because it is the best and truest way to happiness. Every one would think it worth his while to maintain this error and to propagate it."—He continued, " I wish you and other divines would write small pamphlets, to acquaint the people with the advantages of christianity, which might be of greater service than preaching.—In this manner Voltaire has written, as you know, innumerable little pieces against religion, which contain always the same over again under different titles, and in a different dress. Rational friends of christianity should learn of him this method, by which he does much mischief, and apply it to better purposes. Voltaire

boasts

boafts of having found out this method, as he fays, to enlighten the world. I remember that when I converfed with D'Alembert at Paris, in my travels, that he fi oke much in praife of this method, and admired Voltaire's wifdom in this point. However, I do not believe him to be the inventor of it. Perhaps he has borrowed this way of fpreading his principles from Chrift himfelf, who taught truth, fometimes in parables, fometimes in queftions and anfwers, fometimes in fermons."

" D'Alembert told me at the fame time, that he had carefully examined chriftianity, and had found nothing againft reafon in it. But the reafon why he did not adopt it was, becaufe he had no inward feelings of it. Thefe feelings were the gift of God, and fince he denied them him, he hoped to be excufed for not having it, and confequently for not being a chriftian."

Laftly, the Count complained of having been for fome time troubled with difagreeable dreams. He wanted to know how far there was any morality in them, and how far they could be charged to men. Being told that they proceeded from the free exertion of the foul during the time we are awake, he faid : " This anfwer fatisfies me, for I never think of thofe things, to which the

dreams

dreams are related. In general, I obferve, that they derive their origin not from fenfations and ideas, which were but lately in my mind, but from fuch as were at a greater diftance of time. Thus, during the firft week of my imprifon-ment, I dreamt of nothing but of my parents, whom I have not feen a long while. It was as if I were in their houfe and their company. Many things 'that happened in their prefence during my infancy, came into my mind again."

The twenty-ninth Conference. April the 20th.

AMONG other things, which were the fubject of this converfation, it was men-tioned, that the nearer and more perfect contem-plation of the works of God in futurity, would be a fource of pure and everlafting joy to the bleffed. The Count then mentioned, " That the contemplation of the works of nature had oftentimes afforded him great fatisfaction, and that it had been the only means of keeping him from atheifm, into which he otherwife certainly fhould have fallen."

An exhortation of advancing in godlinefs, fince his end was fo near, produced the following

declaration

declaration from him : " Thank God," faid he, " I am ready to die, if it fhould be even to-morrow. The freethinkers will fay, I fhould have found within myfelf ftrength enough againft my misfortunes, without applying to religion. They will fay, I fhewed myfelf now a coward, and was for this reafon unworthy of my former profperity. I wifh to God I had not been unworthy of it for other reafons. However, I fhould like to afk thefe gentlemen, in what manner I fhould have found comfort within myfelf? I durft not think on my crimes, on my prefent fituation, on futurity, if I wanted tranquillity of mind. Nothing was left for me but to endeavour to ftupify myfelf and to diffipate my thoughts. But how long would this have lafted in my prefent folitude, and being removed from all opportunities of diffipation? And fuppofe it had been poffible, it would have been of little ufe, for the caufe of fear and anxiety remained always, and would have roufed me frequently from my artificial infenfibility. I tried this method during the firft weeks of my confinement, before I reflected on my condition. I laid for three or more hours together on my bed. My fancy compofed romances, I travelled through the whole world, and my imaginations produced a thoufand pictures to amufe myfelf

with.

with. But at that time I fancied to see many ways of saving my life. I did not know whether and how far, my crimes might be difcovered. A certain circumftance, which deprived me of all my hopes, was then ftill unknown to me. And even then, diffipation would not anfwer the purpofe. If I could dream in this manner perhaps for feveral hours, my terrors and my anxieties would return again. Perhaps fome people will fay, I fhould have exerted my pride, and fhewn, at leaft by my outward conduct, that nothing could humble me. But alas! what a miferable pride is it to have a bad confcience, and to think of dying on a fcaffold!—No, I find it is better to derive my comfort from the only true fource, which is religion. And I wifh that thofe who blame me now for taking fhelter under it, may find in their laft hours the fame tranquillity it affords me. There is but one thing in this world which makes me really and con-tinually uneafy, which is, that I have feduced others to irreligion and wickednefs. I believe I fhould not properly enjoy my future happinefs, if I knew any of thofe I have deluded, would be eternally unhappy. It is therefore my moft fervent wifh, and my own happinefs depends on it, that God would fhew mercy to all thofe, I have by any means turned from him, and call

them

them back to religion and virtue. I pray to God for this fervently."

Some queſtions being aſked concerning his prayers, he ſaid : " He prayed frequently. He held ſoliloquies in his own heart, and excited himſelf to confirm and rectify his ſentiments more and more. He addreſſed himſelf alſo to God, and begged his aſſiſtance for himſelf and his friends."

He deſired me to let him have ſome of Cramer's ſermons, and the *Meſſiah* of Klopſtock. He ſaid, " He had ſeveral times attempted to read this poem, but he never had any taſte for it. Perhaps the fault might have been his own, becauſe he was ignorant of thoſe doctrines of religion it was grounded upon, and never thought them of any importance. Now as he knew more of religion, and thought quite differently, he would try if the poem might produce good ſentiments in his ſoul."

The thirtieth Conference.   April the 21st.

THE Count was now so much altered, that some of his former friends, whom I told of his present turn of thoughts and of his conduct, would scarce believe it. However, I had not the least reason to doubt of the sincerity of either. I do not know for what purpose he should have attempted to deceive me. Besides, dissimulation was no part of his character. All those who had an opportunity of seeing him, found him the same as I did, and I in particular had from the beginning guarded myself against being deceived. His present peace of mind seemed to me in particular a sure proof of the effects of religion upon his heart. Among many observations he made to-day, the following seem to be of some importance.

" I consider it now," said he, " as a kind of folly, that the deists pretend to be offended at the humble appearance Christ and the first teachers of Christianity made. I need not observe, that in relation to God, nothing is either little or great, but cannot help remarking that this humble appearance of Christ was very well

adapted

adapted to the defign of his miffion. The common people took him now to be one of their equals, and placed confidence in him. For this reafon Chrift chofe his Apoftles among the lower clafs of mankind, and the Apoftles converfed moftly with fuch. And even thefe common people were as proper fpectators of their miracles as an affembly of philofophers, as they were all of that nature, that nothing more was required to judge of them, than the natural fenfes and a common fhare of underftanding. A private foldier is perhaps more fit for fuch an obfervation, than a general who has his head full of other things, or thinks it not worth his while to attend to it. The evidence which is given by men of common underftanding in behalf of Chrift's miracles, is therefore worthy of credit. The learned and the philofophers can now confider thefe facts, and examine whether they are real miracles, and then determine how far they are in favour of Chrift and his doctrine."

Laftly, the Count declared, " that he had a fincere love towards God and his Redeemer, that he rejoiced in the bleffings of eternity, though he was not anxious as to the time when he fhould partake of them. The fenfe of his repentance was not fo lively as formerly, fince he could apply the comforts of the Gofpel to quiet his confci-

3ence.

ence. I beg of you," added he, " confider of my fituation, whether you find me as I fhould be. Write to Cramer, and defire him to tell his opinion; I am ready to do what he or you fhall prefcribe."

The Count knew that there was a correfpondence between Cramer and me concerning the progrefs of his converfion; I ufed to communicate to him thofe paffages in Cramer's letters that related to him. He readily made ufe of Cramer's reflexions and doubts. He was very defirous of his letters, and enquired even the very laft morning of his life, if any of his letters had been received which concerned him.

The thirty-firft Conference. April the 24th.

T H E following obfervation of the Count will ferve to give us an idea of his character.

" Do not mind, faid he, if it fhould be faid, you ought to have urged to me arguments which were not fo philofophical and more evangelical ; I affure you that by no other means you would have found accefs to my heart than by thofe you have chofen. There are only three ways which you might have taken : declamation,

ftirring

stirring up the imagination, and cool enquiry. If you had chosen that of declamation, I should have immediately thought, If the man has a good cause, why does he not propose his reasons without any art: if God has a revealed religion, it must stand the test of enquiry; I therefore should have heard you without any emotion. If you had endeavoured to stir up my imagination, you must have done it by filling it with terrible descriptions of eternity. This method would have had still less effect than declamation: I was very sure that after death there was nothing either to hope or fear. Any impression you might have made through fear would soon have worn off, and would have entirely vanished by recollecting my former system. The only way left you was that which you chose, I mean, cool enquiry. I will tell you now what resolution I had taken before you came, and for what reasons I entered into conversation with you. About eight days before your first visit to me, the commander of the castle asked me if I chose to converse with a divine? Thinking, however, that every clergyman would be apt either to preach too much, or tire me with melancholy declamations, I declined the proposal, and said; I and all divines differ very much in opinion, and I have no inclination to dispute. However, I knew

that

that I muſt expect a clergyman to attend me by
order of government, I therefore reſolved to receive him civilly, and to hear him with decency
and compoſure. I intended to declare to him,
at the end of the firſt viſit, that if he was ordered
to ſee me frequently he would be welcome, but
I ſhould beg of him not to entertain any hopes of
converting me, for I was too well convinced of
my own opinion, and ſhould therefore never
enter into any uſeleſs diſputations.—When you
came, my dear friend, I immediately perceived,
that you had no intention to declaim to me in the
ſtile of a preacher, or to fill me with fears and
terrors, and inflame my imagination. You only
deſired me, ſince the matter was of ſo great conſequence, to examine into my own principles,
and the evidence for chriſtianity. I found this
reaſonable, I had time to do it, and fancied I
ſhould, by this enquiry, diſcover that chriſtianity had no foundation, and convince myſelf
more ſtrongly of the truth of my principles. We
begun our conferences with great coolneſs; I read
the books you gave me, though with diffidence,
yet with attention. This did not continue long,
and I could not help perceiving that I had been
miſtaken. It can ſcarcely be believed how much
it has coſt me to own my error, with regard to
myſelf, as well as with regard to you. You may
remember

remember that I did not from the firſt deny that I had acted wrong, and had been unhappy in my former ſituation, and that my conſcience reproached me. But, conſidering my former obſtinacy, it was a great victory over myſelf, to confeſs that my former principles were falſe. To proceed ſo far was only to be done by reaſon. You are the beſt judge why you treated me in the manner you have done; but the ſucceſs entirely juſtifies you: my converſion is, through the grace of God, luckily brought about. In what manner this is effected muſt be indifferent to all but you and I. Senſible chriſtians will rejoice that my ſoul is ſaved, and that you have choſen this method, which, in regard to me, was the only good one."

Towards the end of our converſation I told him, that this week, in all probability, would be the laſt of his life, as I knew that next Saturday ſentence would be pronounced againſt him, and that between the ſentence and the execution of it, there would be very few days. He received this news with his former reſolution and ſerenity.

" I hope, ſaid he, that I ſhall certainly meet my death without ſtupifying fear and anxiety. I am only apprehenſive that you will be much

M   affected

affected by this shocking scene. If it would have no bad effect upon the spectators, I should desire you not to accompany me to the scaffold."

No, said I, dear Count, I am your only friend, and I dare not leave you. I will comfort you with the hope, which I entertain as a certain one, that you shall be happy in eternity: I will assist you under this severe fate; and the only recompence I expect, is to see you die as a christian.

The thirty-second Conference. April the 23d.

THE Count, after asking me why so many who know the precepts of christianity, do neverthelefs not live up to them, related a conversation he had with one of the officers, wherein he attempted to shew, that it was not impossible to practise the laws of christianity. He afterwards desired me to appoint a day when he could receive the sacrament. I imagined that Thursday would be the day of his execution, and as he wished to comply with this solemn institution some time before he suffered, we appointed the Monday following.

The thirty-third Conference. April the 24th.

THE Count had yesterday finished his account of his conversion, and he now delivered it to me.

He assured me he had drawn it up with a kind of anxiety, left he should fay any thing which was not strictly conformable to his former and present principles. This was the reason why he had been so long about it. He was afraid he might not have expressed himself in some places with perspicuity and propriety, since he had not for some years written much in the German language, and never upon such a subject ; besides, he had endeavoured to express himself with concisenefs, for fear of being too prolix. The employment itself had been very agreeable to him, as it had given him an opportunity of recollecting all the arguments by which he had been convinced, and had now found them so strong, that he was confident he would not redeem his life for all his former prosperity, by any action which might contradict his present conviction. He desired me now to read what he had drawn up, to judge whether it answered that intention for which it was written.

I then

I then read the whole before him, and found some obscure passages, expressions and ideas, which might be misunderstood by christians and unbelievers, and made my remarks upon them. Some of these passages he altered with his own hand, some he rather chose to leave as they were.

" I have drawn up, said he, this account, to convince christians, as well as those which are not, and in whose hands this may fall, that I became a christian after mature consideration, and that I die such. I am pretty well acquainted with the turn of thinking of the last, and will prevent them from saying that I turned christian from fear, and weakness of understanding: I must endeavour to convince them, that I have examined the subject, and reasoned upon it, to shew them, for instance, what is my opinion of the mysteries of religion, and why I do not think them contradictory to reason. If such of my readers as are christians should find my ideas not altogether as they should be, or my expressions sometimes improper, I hope they will not be surprized, considering how new these truths are to me, and how little I am qualified to speak or to write about them. You know, my dear friend, how I now believe, without any further reasoning or explanation or insight into the connexion of the
whole

whole fyftem, every thing that Chrift has taught, becaufe his word is fufficient for me."

The Monday following, as I have mentioned already, was appointed for receiving the facrament. I told the Count, that fince it was a folemn action, and at the fame time a public confeffion of his chriftianity, I thought it proper that it fhould be celebrated before fome witneffes, that were known to be true chriftians. He anfwered:

" I wifhed to receive it with Count Brandt, but fince this will be matter of difficulty, I beg of you to intreat the commander of the caftle to be prefent."

The Count did not appear to me to-day to be fo ferene and chearful as he ufed to be. I enquired what could be the reafon of it, and he gave me the following anfwer:

" You know that to-morrow I expect my fentence; this has induced me to reflect on former times. I thought if I had not acted in fuch a manner as I have done, I fhould not have come into this mifery; it has made me rather uneafy: however you may be fure that this uneafinefs will foon pafs over; I have found already fufficient reafon to be above fuch re-

M 3

flexions,

flexions, since they are at present ill-timed and entirely unnecessary.

The thirty-fourth Conference. April the 25th.

" VOluptuousness, said the Count, is the source of all my misfortunes; ambition has only contributed to hasten and complete them. I have told you already, that when I first came into Denmark I intended to cut as great a figure as my situation would permit. I then did not think of obtaining that power, to which I was raised; I could have satisfied myself with being eminent in my profession as a physician. You will find this to be true from what I am going to tell you. I had resolved to leave Altona, to resign my station there. I intended to go to Malaga, and to settle there as a physician, or to make a voyage to the East Indies. I had the following reasons for my first resolution. I was, at the time I took it, rather in ill health, and hoped a milder climate would agree better with me. The notion that the pleasures of voluptuousness would be greater and more pleasing in a warmer climate, were a matter also of some consequence. The many fine things in the East Indies, which I had read in voyages, and which

had

had warmed my imagination, determined me
more for the Eaſt Endies than for Malaga : beſides the great hopes I had of making a fortune,
and ſatisfying thoſe deſires which made me think
at firſt of Malaga. Now a proſpect opened itſelf
to me, of making my fortune in Denmark. I
ſeized on the favourable opportunity. And
why ? I am almoſt aſhamed to ſay it was owing
to an acquaintance procured by a love intrigue
which brought me hither. How greatly muſt I
deteſt my former way of thinking, which made
me follow a wild paſſion which always was blind !
And how much am I now puniſhed for it !"

He was juſt ſpeaking of ſeveral things which
concerned his heart, of his affections towards his
parents and family, of his complying with his
fate, when his council came into the room to
acquaint him with his ſentence. " Good Count,
ſaid he, I bring you bad news." He then pulled
a copy of the ſentence out of his pocket.

" I expected nothing elſe, ſaid the Count; let
me ſee."

He read. I fixed my eyes upon him with
great attention, but I did not obſerve the leaſt

M 4　　　　　　　alteration

alteration in his countenance. After he had read it, he gave it to me. It was as follows:

" In confequence of the Danifh ftatute law, book vi. chapter iv. art. 1. It is hereby declared juft and right, that Count John Frederick Struenfee, for his due punifhment, and that he may be an example to terrify others, has forfeited his honour, his life, and his eftates. He fhall be degraded from his dignity as Count, and all other digities which have been conferred upon him. His coat of arm, which he had as Count, fhall be broken by the common hangman. Likewife fhall John Frederick Struenfee's right hand, and afterwards his head, be cut off, his body fhall be quartered and laid upon the wheel, and his head and his hand fhall be ftuck upon a pole,"

During the time that I was reading this fentence and trembled, he began to talk with compofure with his council, and afked if all the points of his accufations had been regarded in framing his fentence. The counfel anfwered in the affirmative. " And what will be the fate of Brandt?" His fentence is exactly the fame as yours. " And could his council do nothing in order to fave him?" He has faid every thing that could be faid in his favour, but Count
Brandt

Brandt has too much laid to his charge. The Count was more moved at this, than at his own fate. However he foon recollected himfelf, wrote fomething to what he had drawn up for his council, and returned it to him.

When we were alone, I affured him of my fincere compaffion, and exhorted him to fuffer his fate with the patience and fubmiffion of a chriftian.

" I affure you," faid he, " I am very eafy about that. Such punifhments fhould make an impreffion upon others, and therefore they ought to be fevere. I had prepared myfelf for this and more. I thought I might perhaps be broken upon the wheel, and was already confidering whether I could fuffer this kind of death with patience. If I have deferved it, my infamy would not be removed, though thofe difgraceful circumftances were not annexed to it. And if I had not deferved it, which I cannot affert, fenfible people would do me juftice, and I fhould gain in point of honour. And upon the whole, what is honour or infamy in this world to me? My judges had the law before them, and therefore they could not judge otherwife. I confefs my crime is great;

I have

I have violated the Majesty of the King. Many
things I might not have done if I had been sufficiently acquainted with the law—But why did
I neglect it?"

To be sure, said I, you only are to blame.
One of your crimes, of which there is not the
least doubt, is not only a crime against the King's
Majesty, but also against the whole nation,
and it would be looked upon as such in any
other country. That unlawful power which you
usurped to yourself, is likewise a crime against
the constitution of Denmark. And though perhaps you might not think you had been guilty
of high treason on this account, yet the fact is
proved, and the law is clear. He owned all this,
and I was sorry to have said so many disagreeable things to him. He added:

" I must only beg of you to be upon your
guard, lest you should be too much affected
when I go to die. The friendship I have for
you, from which I cannot but sympathize with
you, would make me very uneasy to see you
suffer. Let us however continue our conversation calmly and composed to the last. Upon
the scaffold speak to me as little as possible, and
as you shall think proper. I shall certainly do
as much as lies in my power to direct my thoughts
towards

towards God and my Redeemer. I fhall not take my leave of you. Believe me, that without this ceremony, which likely might difcompofe my mind, I know and feel how much I owe you."

My readers will recollect how much this unhappy man was moved by a letter he received from his father, at a time when he ftill maintained his irreligious principles. Now they have feen with what a compofure of mind he heard his fentence, after he was become a chriftian.

He delivered to me the following letter for his parents, and left it to me, whether I would fend it now or after his death. I chofe the latter, becaufe I knew his execution was very near, and I would fave them the anxiety of expecting the melancholy news of it. The letter was as follows:

" Your letters have encreafed my pain, but I have found in them that love which you always expreffed for me. The memory of all that forrow which I have given you, by living contrary to your good advice, and the great affliction my imprifonment and death muft caufe you,
grieves

grieves me the more, since, enlightened by truth, I see clearly the injury I have done. With the most sincere repentance, I beg your pardon and forgiveness. I owe my present situation to my belief in the doctrine and redemption of Christ. Your prayers and your good example have contributed much towards it. Be assured, that your son has found that great good, which you believe to be the only true one. Look upon his misfortune as the means which made him obtain it. All impressions which my fate could make upon you, will be weakened by this, as it has effaced them with me. I recommend myself to your further intercession before God. I pray incessantly to Christ my Redeemer, that he may enable you to bear your present calamities. I owe the same to his assistance. My love to my brother and sisters. I am, with all filial respect, &c."

The thirty-fifth Conference. April the 26th.

I Heard from General lieutenant Holben, the commander of the castle, that Struensee had been very uneasy all last night: That he had kicked with his feet, gnashed with his teeth, and gnawed his fingers. The officer upon guard got up to him, but found him fast asleep. I

enquired

enquired of my unfortunate friend, whether he had been troubled with disagreeable dreams. He said:

" That when he awaked in the morning, he remembered nothing but the bringing to his memory all the arguments, by which he was convinced of the truth of christianity. Of the uneasiness of his body he remembered nothing."

I had to acquaint him with the melancholy news that his sentence was confirmed in every particular circumstance, and that it was to be executed the day after to-morrow. I hoped he would hear it with a composed mind, and it happened so. As to those circumstances which were to throw infamy upon his death, he expressed himself thus:

" I am far above all this, and I wish my friend Brandt may be the same. Here in this world, since I am on the point of leaving it, neither honour nor infamy can affect me any more. It is equally the same to me after death, whether my body putrifies under ground or in the open air, whether it serves to feed the worms or the birds. God will know very well how to preserve those particles of my body, which, on the day of resurrection, are to constitute my future glorified

glorified body. It is not my all which is to be laid upon the wheel. Thank God! I know now very well that this duſt is not my whole being."

When I told him that next Tueſday would be his dying day, he anſwered:

" I thought it would be Friday. However, I do not wiſh even for this ſhort delay. It would be the ſame as if I was to undergo a painful operation for my health, and ſhould deſire to have it delayed when it was juſt going to be performed. I ſhould be obliged to ſubmit to it at laſt, and I ſhould only recover my health later."—He then went through all the circumſtances of his death, and compared them with thoſe of the death of Chriſt, and found that Jeſus had ſuffered infinitely more for his ſake, than he was to ſuffer on account of his crimes. He praiſed the power of prayer in comforting him, when he was now and then anxious about the ſtep he was to take.

I am unable to deſcribe the eaſe and tranquillity with which he ſpoke. I expected much from the power of religion over his heart, but it exceeded my moſt ſanguine expectations.

He

He affured me that religion, and his firm hopes of being pardoned by God, had produced this eafe of mind. He owned that his natural coolnefs of temper, his ufing himfelf for many years to keep his imagination within bounds, and his entertaining himfelf rather with reflections of found reafon than images of fancy, had in fome refpects fupported him; but he was convinced that all this, without religion, would never have compofed his mind. God had adapted it for all kind of tempers and for all characters. It was fit for all men, and it found in him a good foil to produce all its good effects of tranquillity and fortitude in adverfity. He added: " Although the way which leads me out of this world is very difagreeable, yet I have reafon to praife God that he has made choice of it; that he has fhewn me the approaching death aforehand, and at the fame time has extricated me out of the pleafures and diffipations of this life. In no other manner fhould I have become acquainted with truth, or fhould have reformed my fentiments; though I am fure I fhould have adopted chriftianity in all fituations of life, if I had known it fo well as I do now : And yet, I never fhould have taken proper time to examine into it. When I formerly thought on death, it had but little effect upon me. I rather

fuppreffed

suppreſſed it, ſometimes by thinking it was a fate which could not be avoided, and therefore was not to be called into our thoughts before there was occaſion for it: ſometimes, by perſuading myſelf it was folly to imbitter the preſent enjoyments, by thinking on what was to come. Even when I was in danger of my life, I avoided looking into futurity. I have been ſometimes ſo dangerouſly ill, that my life has been deſpaired of; I have been riding furiouſly, and no longer ago than laſt ſummer broke my arm, by being thrown from my horſe, but it never entered my thoughts to look one ſtep further than this preſent life.

Being reminded of ſelf-examination, he ſaid, " he did it every day. It was an occupation he liked."——Among other things, he ſaid: " I know my adminiſtration of ſtate affairs is very blameable before God and men, and my own conſcience, on account of the bad principles by which I was actuated, namely, levity, haſte, pride and ſelfiſhneſs. How far they are wrong, either upon the whole or ſingly conſidered in a political light, I am unable indeed to determine, becauſe I ſhall not live to ſee the conſequences. However, I muſt expect to have been ſubject to error in my political principles, as well as I

have

have been in my religious ones. I leave this point to be decided by thofe that furvive me, and I fubmit to their judgment. This only I can and muft fay, (for I fhould fpeak untruth if I was to fpeak othetwife) that I am not con-fcious of any bad intentions."

After this a converfation enfued about the Lord's Supper. When it was finifhed, I told him that a poor peafant, who met me to-day in the ftreet, called out to me: ' Father, do what you can to convince Struenfee that he has finned againft our Lord Jefus Chrift; and if he ac-knowledges this he will be faved.' The Count was much pleafed, on account of the chriftian love which this man had fhewn; and obferved that chriftianity could inftill fentiments of humanity into the minds of illiterate people whofe fouls were not refined by education.

" Reading," faid he, " will not fufficiently entertain me at prefent, therefore I have been writing to-day." Among the reft he had written the following letter to Lady Perkentin at Pinneberg, which he defired me to take care that it might be fafely delivered. The following is the letter.

N

My

My Lady,

" I make use of the first moments, which permit me to write to you. Business, duties, and my late connexions, have perhaps lessened in me the remembrance of my former friends, but they have not been able to obliterate their memory entirely. My present leisure has revived it the more lively. If my silence has raised suspicion against my former sentiments, I beg pardon of all those that are intitled to my gratitude, and of you, my Lady, in particular. This, however, is not the only advantage, which the change of my fate has produced. I owe my knowledge of truth to it, it has procured me a happiness of which I had no more expectation, since I had already lost sight of it. I intreat you to consider my misfortunes in no other light but that of religion. I gain more by it than ever I can lose, and I feel and assure you of this with conviction, ease and joy of heart. I beg of you to repeat what I now write, in the house of Count Ahlefeld and at Ranzau. I am under great obligations to these two families, and it has grieved me the more, to have drawn with me into misfortunes, persons which are related to them. Permit me, my Lady, to

add

add to this, my respects to Lady Thun, and the family of Mr. de Waitz. I remain, with most respectful sentiments, &c."

April the 26th, 1772.

The thirty-fifth Conference. April the 26th.

I Came to-day to the Count with general lieutenant Hoben, who, at my request, was present at his receiving the sacrament. I administered it to him; and this man, who received his sentence of death without any appearing alteration of mind, was during the whole time of this sacred transaction, as if he was melting into tears. I never observed a tear in his eyes as often as we were talking about his misfortunes and death; but on account of his sins, his moral misery into which he had thrown himself and others; on account of the love of God towards him and all mankind, he has wept more than I myself should believe, if I had not seen it.

When the whole transaction of receiving the sacrament was over, he begged leave of the commander of the castle, to make presents of the trifles that he had left, his bed, his linen,

and

and the little money which he had faved out of his allowance, which was a rixdollar or a crown every day. He faid, " I have now no more property."

He then took his farewel of the commander, in a very affecting manner; thanked him for all kindnefs he had fhewn him, and declared, that he had not denied him any favour that was in his power to grant. The old venerable man left him with thefe words: " I am fure we fhall find one another again before the throne of God."

When we were alone again, he faid: " Nothing is now of great importance to me, but to be certain, that I fhall appear before God with all poffible fincerity and uprightnefs of fentiment. I therefore have examined myfelf once more carefully, and I find a kind of pleafure in it, becaufe it is my duty. I am confcious that I perform every thing chearfully and without the leaft reluctance, fince, enlightened by chriftianity, I have learnt what is my duty. Thus have I thought myfelf obliged, to draw up the account of my converfion, which is in your poffeffion, to efface as much as poffible that impreffion, which I have made upon others by my
converfation

converfation and example. I can affure you, I felt more fatisfaction in writing it, than ever I did in drawing up other things, that concerned partly my defence. I have more minutely examined my adminiftration of ftate affairs; and I can, according to my confcience, judge of it no otherwife than I told you yefterday. I go into eternity, confcious that it was not my intention to make the King or the nation unhappy. It is true, I have, within a fhort time, amaffed confiderable riches, and taken advantage of the King's favour towards me, in a manner I cannot anfwer for; but I never have falfified the accounts, though much in this refpect feems to be againft me, and I can blame nobody who thinks me in this refpect likewife culpable."

It is difficult to difmifs every fufpicion on this head againft Struenfee. And if he was guilty, of how little value would be his converfion! It has made me uneafy frequently, and even now ftill after his death. All manner of appearances, his own confeffion, that he could not free himfelf from all fufpicion, and many other evidences are againft him. However, on the other fide, it makes me eafy that he confeffed greater and more punifhable crimes, without

N 3

conftraint,

conftraint, but denied this with a firmnefs, calmnefs of mind and confidence, which, in-explicable as the matter remains, makes it difficult to believe him guilty.

" I have traced out, continued he, the origin from which my prefent calmnefs and tranquillity proceeds. I am fure they are quite different from thofe which afforded me comfort in my former misfortunes. It is quite impoffible in my prefent fituation, to draw my thoughts from my imminent danger by diffipation. Approach-ing death is not fo eafily expelled from one's thoughts. I feel no more of any pride. I am too fenfible how little I am in this my prifon. I deteft the principle that teaches, there are no ex-pectations after death. Nothing but the affurance of the divine mercy through faith in Chrift, and the confcioufnefs that I fpare no pains to make my fentiments acceptable before God, comforts and compofes me."

" However," added he, " this my eafe makes me not idle; for I continue, and fhall do fo until to the very laft, to fearch earneftly after all thofe things in me which ftill may difpleafe God, that I may remove them as much as poffible."

3

Among

Among the many proofs he gave of this, I shall only mention the following, becaufe it fhews how fcrupuloufly confcientious he was.

" I think, faid he, that it is the duty of a chriftian to pray before he fits down to a meal, though my fentiments in this refpect do not favour fuperftition. It is but juft, to direct our thoughts on fuch occafions, full of gratitude, towards him who fupplies our wants in this way. I therefore have made it for fome time a rule to pray before and after dinner and fupper. However, my old cuftom had frequently fo much power over me, that I oftentimes fat down to eat before I had faid grace. Now it may be equally the fame whether I direct my thoughts towards God, before or after having taken two or three fpoonfuls of foup; but it has vexed me to find that my old carelefs way of thinking has made me forget, what I thought to be my duty."

How do my readers like the confcientioufnefs of a man, who formerly indulged himfelf in every thing his paffions drove him to?

N

The thirty-seventh Conference. April the 27th.

I Found him to-day in the moſt unfeigned tranquillity of mind, to which indeed I had been witneſs for ſeveral weeks paſt, but which appeared more and more ſtriking to me the nearer the time of his death advanced. I praiſed God in my heart, who ſhewed ſo much mercy to this unhappy man! How often did I wiſh that I might not be the only man upon earth, who heard him ſpeak ſo compoſedly about his death.

He had written another letter to the Chamberlain de Brandt, the brother of the unhappy Count, which he deſired me to get delivered. Several other papers, which he had written in his priſon, were incloſed in a cover, and ſealed up by me in the preſence of the commander of the caſtle, who once more did us the favour to come into the priſon. The other papers, which conſiſted of thoſe writings of mine, which I had given him from time to time, and the two letters of his parents to him, he delivered to me likewiſe.—And now he had ſet his houſe in order.—

The

The following · is the letter to the Chamberlain de Brandt.

 " Sir,

"Permit me to bewail with you and the Lady your mother, the fate of our dear Enevold. Do not think me unworthy, of sharing this your grief with you, though accidentally I have been the cause of it. You know how much I love him. He was the man of all the world who poſſeſſed the largeſt ſhare of my friendſhip. His misfortunes give me the greateſt anxiety, and my own have been on this account moſt painful to me. He has ſhared my proſperity with me, and I truſt that we now both together ſhall enjoy that happineſs which our Redeemer has promiſed us. I do not know any thing wherewith I could comfort you. You are acquainted with religion. There I found refuge to comfort me on account of my misfortune. I pray to God, that he in this very moment will let you feel all its power. I ſhall not ceaſe to entertain a moſt lively ſenſe of gratitude for all thoſe perſons, which are dear to me at Ranzau. I am wholly your's."

April the 27th, 1772.

" *P. S.* I have been in hopes, and ſtill flatter myſelf, that the ſentence of my friend will be mitigated."

The ſubject of our to-day's conversation was chiefly upon the redemption of Chriſt. I repeated moſtly what I had ſpoken on the ſubject already when we purpoſely treated on it. He ſaid many ſtriking and edifying things on this occaſion; but the emotion my heart was in, prevented my perfect remembrance of each particular. The following is part of it

"I look upon the reconciliation of men to God, through the death of Chriſt, as the only means of receiving forgiveneſs of ſins. Every thing elſe, which is believed to ſerve the ſame purpoſe, is apparently inſufficient. But this is conformable to all our notions of God; it produces ideas ſuitable to the attributes of God; it is founded on the beſt reaſons, and procures us comfort and chearfulneſs at the time when death approaches. Whoever will not adopt and make uſe of this redemption, declares that he will neither be virtuous, nor fear God; for he rejects the ſtrongeſt motives which God could ever propoſe to mankind, to fear him and to love virtue; he ſlights the aſſiſtance of God, without which nobody can be honeſt or good."

He added: "I leave the world, fully convinced of the truth of the chriſtian religion."
I then

I then turned our conversation upon the love of a pious christian towards God, I shewed him how much we were obliged to this love on account of the redemption, and asked him how he found his love towards God and his Redeemer. He said:

" I look upon God and Christ as my best friends; and in this view I consider those obligations of love which I owe to God and my Redeemer. I first must know and feel for what I am indebted to my friend and benefactor. He is desirous of making me happy, he finds the means of doing it, he sacrifices on my account what he loves and what is dear to him, As long as I do not acknowledge this, or do not know how to value the same, so long am I unworthy of his friendship, and do not love him. I am further obliged to shew my readiness to act according to his intentions : else I am ungrateful, and want him to be my friend only for self-interest, and to do nothing myself that was worthy of his friendship. You see here the principles according to which I love God and my Redeemer. I know what God has done for me, and what it has cost Christ to procure my salvation. I know how great the blessing is which I shall enjoy through him. But I am likewise
conscious

conscious that I do, whatever I can, to act according to the will of God, to rectify my sentiments, and to prepare myself for death in a manner which may be acceptable before God. I submit without the least reluctance to his will in regard to myself, because I know he loves me. I look upon my death, and all those awful and ignominious circumstances that are to attend it, as things which God found necessary for my own good. In the beginning of my confinement, I thought quite different from what I do now, even when I recollected that my affairs might perhaps turn out in the manner that they do now. I wished to fall sick and to die. I even had the thought of abstaining from eating and to starve myself to death: yet I never should have laid hands on myself, though I should have had an opportunity for it. I now praise God heartily that neither of the two has taken place."

I told him, that these sentiments gave me great satisfaction in regard to his salvation, and that I saw now how great reason he had to be so calm and so composed as I found him.

" Yes, thanks be to God, said he, I am as satisfied as a man can be who sees his greatest happiness before him. I therefore humbly adore

the

the mercy of God, and the power of religion. If it happens that my tranquillity is interrupted for fome moments, it is caufed by the wifh to be convinced that I have fulfilled all thofe conditions under which God will grant me mercy, and that I am fuch as God wants me to be. I therefore have taken the book of Spalding into my hands again, to fatisfy myfelf on this point." I anfwered,

That I did not know of any other conditions of our falvation, and the Bible taught us no other but thefe two: an unlimited confidence in God through Chrift, and a zeal to think and to act always according to the will of God. And fince he was confcious that he believed in Chrift, and that he loved God, he had no reafon to doubt of his being pardoned before God. He then faid:

" I have examined myfelf in all refpects I could think of, and I find nothing that can make me uneafy. If I found any thing of this kind, I fhould have told you of it, and have afked your advice. But how eafily may I have overlooked many things which are known to God; and if fo, what will he do?"

He

He will forgive you, said I, becaufe you have done what you could do in thofe circumftances you were in. We cannot raife ourfelves to per-fection.

We afterwards confulted and fettled how we fhould act to-morrow, it being the day when he was to die. I promifed to be with him fome hours before he went to the fcaffold; for, ac-cording to the King's order, I durft not go along with him to the place of execution; I was to go before him, and to receive him there.

He defired me to carry on our converfation to-morrow, as compofedly and as coolly as hitherto. He wifhed that we might finifh what we had to do on the fcaffold as quick as poffible, and that I might keep up my fpirits, that he might not fee me fuffer. As for himfelf, he fhould fay nothing there but what he thought abfolutely neceffary; for he would direct his thoughts entirely towards God, and that eternity he was to enter into.

I told him, that according to the ritual I was to afk him a great many queftions, but that I thought I had a right of fhortening them. I did this in his prefence, wrote the queftions down,

which

which I was to afk him, and read them to him afterwards.

" I do not chufe, faid he, to fee my brother and to take leave of him, on account of the tendernefs of our fituation. I beg therefore of you to do it in my name. I intreat his pardon, for drawing him with me into misfortunes, but I hope and am certain that his affairs will turn out well. I affure him of my leaving this world with true brotherly affection for him. Tell him likewife of the fentiments in which I die, and how you find me."

This commiffion, which was the moft tender and moft moving I ever had, I difcharged, by the leave of the commander, this very evening, and carried back the anfwer of the much affected brother.

The thirty-eighth Conference. April the 28th.

ACcording to the account of the officer who had the watch that night, the Count, who now was certainly no more an unhappy man, had been reading a good while the preceeding evening,

and

and went to bed pretty early. He had flept for five or fix hours together very foundly. When he wakened in the morning, he had fpent a good while in deep meditation. He then got up, dreffed himfelf, and converfed with the officer very compofedly.

I found him lying on a couch, dreffed as he intended to go to the place of execution. He was reading Shlegel's fermons on the fufferings of Chrift, and received me with his ufual ferene and compofed countenance. He faid :

" I was thinking laft night whether it might not ftrengthen me in my way to death, if I was to fill my fancy with agreeable images of eternity and future blifs. I might have ufed for this purpofe *Lavater's Profpeƈts into Eternity:* but I will not venture to do this. I rather think it better to take this great ftep in cool confideration. Fancy, if once put in agitation, can foon take a falfe turn. It could difmifs (perhaps) at once, my agreeable and pleafing profpeƈts of eternity, and eagerly catch at the formidable circumftances of death, by which means I fear that I fhould be unmanned. Even in going to the place of execu-tion, I will not indulge it, but rather employ my

reafon

reafon in meditating on the walk of Chrift to his death, and apply it to myfelf."

He then defired me, if I thought it neceffary, to affure his judges in his name once more, that what he had confeffed, was in all refpects the truth, and that he had not wilfully concealed any thing, which he himfelf or others could be charged with. He continued :

" When I awoke this morning and found that it was daylight, my whole body was feized with a vehement trembling. I took directly to prayer, and confidered the comforts of religion. I prayed for the King, that God's wifdom and mercy might guide him, and that he perfonally might be perfectly happy. I foon recovered my fpirits again. I am now calm and com-pofed, and I am fure I fhall remain fo. Why fhould I make myfelf uneafy, when I am fully convinced of my falvation ? God has forgiven me my fins, and even thofe which I do not re-member; he has pardoned me for thofe things which he ftill diflikes in me, and which I by felf-examination could not difcover, and therefore could not reform. God can not forgive vice in general, without doing the fame in every parti-cular fpecies of vice. The remembrance of the

O   fufferings

fufferings of Chrift, who has fatisfied God for all men, affure me of this. And fince I am fo certain of my falvation, I do not dread death. Fear of death would be inconfiftent under circumftances fo full of a happy eternity. Befides, I cannot complain that my fate is too hard. I know that I deferve this and ftill more. But, "who fhall lay any thing to the charge of God's elect?—Who is he that condemneth?"

I took the opportunity he gave me, to explain to him the whole eighth chapter of St. Paul to the Romans: There were fo many beautiful paffages which were excellently well adapted to his former and his prefent fituation. The moft vifible calmnefs was to be obferved in his whole countenance ; and he frequently prevented my going on, by falling into the fame obfervations I was juft going to make in order to ftrengthen his faith.

He now afked me: " How far am I permitted to keep up my fortitude by natural means? For inftance : by endeavouring to retain prefence of mind, and not to permit myfelf to be carried away by imagination and fancy." I anfwered,

If

If God has given you a certain ftrength of foul, it is his will that you fhall make ufe of it, in thofe moments when you ftand moft in need of it. But no inward pride or any ill-founded complacency is to interfere. You are to do nothing merely for the fake of being applauded by the fpectators on account of your refolution and compofure. You are to be above fuch things. God loves fincerity, which confifts in fhewing ourfelves outwardly as we are inwardly. Shew yourfelf therefore exactly in the manner as you feel yourfelf within. If you even fhould be fo much affected as to fhed tears, do not hide them, and do not be afhamed of them ; for they are no difhonour to you. You cannot conceal from yourfelf, even unto the very laft moment of your life, why you are to die. You would do wrong, and offend true chriftians, if you were to die with a chearfulnefs, which can only fall to the fhare of thofe that fuffer for the fake of truth and virtue. I wifh to fee you on the fcaffold with vifible figns of repentance and forrow, but at the fame time with a peace of mind which arifes from a confidence of being pardoned before God. I fhould even diflike to fee you conceal the natural fear of death. He faid :

" I am certainly not inclined to make any fhew before men. Nothing can be now more inte-

refting

resting to me than to please God, and to conquer the terrors of death. If I should force myself to appear outwardly different from what I am within, it would happen to me what happens to a man, who is to speak to an eminent person, and has well considered every thing he is going to say, but now begins to stammer, and, by endeavouring to prevent this, becomes quite speechless. I shall, as much as lies in my power, direct my thoughts towards God, and not disturb myself by studying to satisfy the expectation of the spectators. Therefore I shall say nothing on the scaffold, but what you yourself shall give me occasion for."

I assure you, said I, I shall give you very few opportunities for it; the scaffold is neither for you nor for me the place for speaking much. When you are there, it will be your business to strengthen your thoughts as much as possible, forgetting those things which are behind, and reaching forth unto those things which are before.

" Now, said he, since I am so near death, I find how necessary and how beneficial to men the positive assertion of Christ is of the existence of eternity. If I was not sure of this, mere reason would give me but little satisfaction upon this question : Whether a few hours hence any thing would

would be left of me that retained its life ?—I can likewife tell you, from my prefent experience, that a bad confcience is worfe than death. I now find comfort againft death, but as long as the former lafted, I had no peace within me. I believe that I fhould have become quite hardened, if this wound had not been healed."

" I believe you have obferved, that I would not let thofe fenfations which were produced by my certainty of being pardoned before God, grow very lively. They might have hindered me in my ftudying to reform my heart, and in examining myfelf. But now I enjoy the comfort of being confcious to have done what I could to pleafe God."

In the abovementioned letter to the chamberlain de Brandt, he had faid that he had become innocently the caufe of his brother's misfortunes. He defired me to explain thefe words to him : " That he, with a good intention, had brought his friend Brandt to Copenhagen, and had kept him from withdrawing himfelf when he had a good opportunity for it."

Now the door of the prifon opened, for which the Count himfelf never, but I very often, had looked with a fearful expectation.—An officer

came

came in, and defired me, if I pleafed, to ftep into the coach, and to go before the Count to the place of execution. I was much moved and affected. The Count, as if it did not concern him in the leaft, comforted me by faying:

" Make yourfelf eafy, my dear friend, by con-fidering the happinefs I am going to enter into, and with the confcioufnefs that God has made you a means of procuring it for me."

I embraced him, recommending him to the love and mercy of God, and haftened to the place of execution.

He being foon called after me, got up from his couch, and followed thofe which were to con-duct him. Coming out of the prifon and getting into the coach, he bowed to thofe that were ftanding around. Upon the way to the place of execution, he partly fpoke to the officer who was with him in the coach, partly fat in deep medi-tation.

As foon as both the condemned were arrived in their refpective coaches near the fcaffold, and Count Brandt had mounted it firft, I got into the coach of Struenfee, and ordered the coach-man to turn about, to prevent his having the profpect of the fcaffold.

" I have

" I have seen him already," said he. I could not recollect myself so soon, and he finding my uneasiness, said, with a smiling countenance, " Pray do not mind me. I see you suffer. Remember that God has made you an instrument in my conversion. I can imagine how pleasing it must be to you to be conscious of this. I shall praise God with you in eternity that you have saved my soul."

I was still more affected than before, and said, that I should look upon this transaction of mine as the most remarkable one during my whole life, since God had blessed it with so self-rewarding a success. It was a pleasing thought to me, that we should continue our friendship in a future world.—I should have comforted him, but he, in this case, comforted me. He desired me then to remember him to several of his acquaintance, and to tell some of them, that if he, by his conversation and actions, had misled them in their notions of virtue and religion, he, as a dying man, acknowledged the injury he had done, begged them to efface these impressions, and to forgive him.

After some silence on both sides, he asked me: " Suppose God, since he knows all things, should see that in case I had lived longer, I should

not

not have kept faithfully to my prefent principles
and fentiments; could that have any influence
upon that judgment which I fhall foon receive?"
I anfwered,

God judges by actions that are committed,
not by thofe that are not. He judges men according as he finds them when they leave this
world. He is love itfelf, and has no pleafure in
the death of him that dieth. He certainly will
not condemn any one who dies in fulfilling
thofe conditions under which he has promifed
his pardon. He then continued:

" It is true, I returned late to God, but I know
that he who is from eternity, cares not for the
length or fhortnefs of time in which man has endeavoured to pleafe him. Our Saviour fays,
without determining any thing relative to this
matter, " He that comes to me, I will in no wife
caft out;" I therefore will make myfelf eafy that
I have kept fo long from God and virtue."

On feeing the great number of fpectators, I
told him, that among thefe thoufands, were
many that would pray to God to have mercy
upon him.

" I hope fo, faid he, and the thought pleafes
me." He foon after added:

I   " It

" It is a solemn sight to see so many thousands of people together; but what are these
thousands, when compared with the whole sum
of all God's creatures, and how very little appears one single man in such a comparison?
Nevertheless God loves every individual man so
much, that he has procured his salvation by sacrificing his own son. What a love is this!

" You see me, continued he, outwardly, the
same as I find myself within." And I perceived, all
the while I was sitting with him in the coach, no
alteration, but that he was pale, and that it was
more difficult for him to think and to converse
than it was some days before, or even this very
morning. However, he had his full presence of
mind, knew several of those that stood about the
coach, bowed to many by pulling off his hat,
and to some he bowed with a friendly mien.

" My ease, said he, is not a forced one. I
cannot recollect any cause from which this ease
arises, that could displease God. I am not ambitious to gain the applause of men, and I do
not promise that I shall not shew any uneasiness
upon the scaffold. I now have disagreeable sensations, and I shall have more there, which I will
not endeavour to conceal. But you may be
assured, that my soul will look with calmness

and

and hope beyond death. And how little is that which I am going to fuffer, when I compare it with the fufferings Chrift bore when he died. Recollect only his words: " My God, my God, why haft thou forfaken me?" and confider, what excruciating pain it muft have caufed him, to hang for feveral hours on the crofs before he died!"

I exhorted him again not to fhew any affected fortitude in thefe laft moments which was not natural to him. Such affectations would certainly difpleafe God, and if he now ftill would mind what the fpectators might think, I muft tell him, that only a few fhort-fighted people would believe his affected firmnefs to be true.

I then faid: Chrift prayed for his murderers even on the crofs. May I rely upon your leaving this world with the fame fentiments of love towards thofe you might have reafon to think your enemies ?

" Firft, faid he, I hope that there is no one who has a perfonal hatred againft me ; but that thofe who have promoted my misfortunes, have done it with an intent of doing good. Secondly, I look upon myfelf already as a citizen of ano-

ther

ther world, and that I am obliged to entertain sentiments conformable to this dignity : and I am sure, that if I was to see those, who might perhaps be my enemies, here in the bliss of that world which I hope to enter into, it would give me the highest satisfaction. I pray to God that if my enemies might repent of their behaviour towards me, this repentance may induce them to look out for that salvation which I promise myself through the mercy of God."

Though I could not see the scaffold, yet I guessed, from the motion of the spectators, that it was Struensee's turn to mount it. I endeavoured to prepare him for it by a short prayer, and within a few moments we were called. He passed with decency and humbleness through the spectators, and bowed to some of them. With some difficulty he mounted the stairs. When we came up, I spoke very concisely, and with a low voice, upon these words of Christ : " He that believeth in me, though he were dead, yet shall he live." It would have been impossible for me to speak much and loud, even if I had attempted it.

I observe here that he shewed not the least affectation in his conduct upon the scaffold : I
found

found him to be one who knew that he was to die, on account of his crimes, by the hands of the executioner. He was pale, it was difficult for him to fpeak, the fear of death was vifible in his whole countenance; but at the fame time, fubmiffion, calmnefs and hope were expreffed in his air and deportment.

His fentence, and afterwards the King's con-firmation of it, were read to him; his coat of arms was publickly fhewn and broken to pieces. During the time that his chains were taking off, I put the following queftions to him: Are you truly forry for all thofe actions by which you have offended God and men?

" You know my late fentiments on this point, and I affure you they are this very moment ftill the fame."

Do you truft in the redemption of Chrift, as the only ground of your being pardoned before God?

" I know no other means of receiving God's mercy, and I truft in this alone."

Do you leave this world without hatred or malice againft any perfon whatever?

" I hope

"I hope nobody hates me perfonally; and as for the reft, you know my fentiments on this head, they are the fame as I told you juft before."

I then laid my hand upon his head, faying: Then go in peace whither God calls you! His grace be with you!

He then began to undrefs, and enquired of the executioners how far he was to uncover himfelf, and defired them to affift him. He then haftened towards the block, that was ftained and ftill reeking with the blood of his friend, laid himfelf quickly down, and endeavoured to fit his neck and chin properly into it. When his hand was cut off, his whole body fell into convulfions. The very moment when the executioner lifted up the axe to cut off his hand, I began to pronounce flowly the words; "Remember Jefus Chrift crucified, who died, but is rifen again." Before I had finifhed thefe words, both hand and head, fevered from the body, lay before my feet.

*　*　*　*　*　*

How wonderful is God, and how great his care for the falvation of men, that are ftill capable of being faved! But how different is the judgment we are to pronounce over fuch men, according

according to the principles of the kingdom of
God, from that which the world pronounces!
If Count Struenfee had remained in his former
profperity, and died a natural death, he might
have been called a great and enlightened man
through all ages, even if he had been at the bottom
the greateft villain. The world has feen him die a
malefactor; but the difpofition in which he left
the world, will be a fufficient inducement for true
chriftians to forgive him the ignominy wherewith he had ftained his life, and to praife God
that he died well.

COUNT STRUENSEE's

OWN ACCOUNT

How he came to alter his Sentiments of

RELIGION.

WRITTEN WITH HIS OWN HAND.

To Dr. MUNTER.

YOU defire, dear friend, that I fhould leave behind me * my thoughts, how I was induced to alter my fentiments in regard to religion. You have been witnefs of it. You have been my guide, and therefore I am infinitely obliged to you. I fatisfy your defire with fo much greater pleafure, as it will afford me an opportunity of recollecting the train of ideas and impreffions of mind which have produced my prefent fentiments, and confirm my prefent conviction.

My unbelief and my averfion to religion, were founded neither upon an accurate inquiry into its truth, nor upon a critical examination of thofe doubts that are generally made againft it. They arofe, as is ufual in fuch cafes, from a very general and fuperficial knowledge of religion on one fide, and much inclination to difobey it's precepts on the other, together with a readinefs to entertain every objection which I difcovered

* The reader will recollect what is faid about this account in the Preface, and p. 142, 143, 163, 164.

P

againft

againſt it. You know how indifferent that common inſtruction in religion is, which is given in public ſchools : yet I was to blame not to have made uſe of the private inſtructions and example of my parents. Since my fourteenth year, all my time was taken up in ſtudying phyſic. If I afterwards ſpent much time in reading other books, it was only to divert myſelf, and to extend my knowledge of thoſe ſciences by means of which I hoped to make my fortune. The violence of the paſſions which made me abandon myſelf in my youth to all ſenſual pleaſures and extravagancies, left me ſcarce time to think of morality, much leſs of religion.

When experience afterwards taught me how little ſatisfaction was to be found in the irregular enjoyment of ſuch pleaſures, and reflection convinced me that a certain inward ſatisfaction was requiſite for my happineſs, ſuch as cannot be attained either by the obſervance of particular duties, or by the omiſſion of ſcandalous exceſſes : I therefore endeavoured to imprint in my mind ſuch principles as I judged proper to govern my actions, and which I thought would anſwer the end I had in view. But how did I undertake this taſk ? My memory was filled up with moral principles, but at the ſame time, I

had

had various excuses to reconcile a complying reason with the weaknesses and the infirmities of the human heart. My understanding was prepossessed with doubts and difficulties, against the infallibility of those means by which we arrive at truth and certainty. My will was (if not fully determined, yet) secretly much inclined to comply only with such duties, as did not lay me under the necessity of sacrificing my favourite inclinations. These were my guides in my researches.

I took it for granted, that in matters merely relative to the happiness of man, neither a deep understanding nor wit or learning were required; but our own experience and ideas only, of which every one must be conscious, were sufficient to find out the truth. The necessity of avoiding all disagreeable sensations of pain, of sickness, of reproaches, as well our own as those of others, made me think that an exact observation of duties towards myself and my neighbour, were of the greatest consequence. However, I believed, from the consideration of God and the nature of man, that there were no particular obligations towards the supreme Being, besides those which are derived from the admiration of

P 2   his

his greatnefs and the general gratitude on account of our exiſtence. The actions of man, as far as they are determined by notions produced by natural inſtincts, by agreeable or diſagreeable impreſſions of external objects, of education, of cuſtom, and the different circumſtances he is in, appear to me to be ſuch, as could in particular inſtances neither pleaſe nor diſpleaſe God, any more than the different events in nature, which are founded in its eternal laws. I was ſatisfied in obſerving that general as well as particular inſtances, tended to one point, namely the preſervation of the whole; and this alone was what I thought worthy of the care of a ſupreme Being. My attention therefore was chiefly fixed upon the duties I owed to my neighbours. The obſervance of which would as well promote my outward happinefs, as give me inward ſatisfaction.

The deſire which every one feels to be virtuous, and a natural inclination for actions uſeful in ſociety, induced me to uſe my utmoſt endeavours to acquire a habit of virtue. But how could I find out true virtue, as I did not ſeek for it, where it was only to be found? What a difference is there in the opinions of philoſophers

phers about its nature and its motives; how contradicting is the judgment of men on account of
the effects it produces in particular cafes! Yet
thefe were to determine my method of acting,
even if God did not judge me, and I fhould
refign myfelf up to my confcience, which is fo
eafily mifled, fo often overpowered by paffions,
and fo frequently not to be heard at all. I
found at leaft, how eafy it was to deceive ourfelves in regard to our fentiments, though they
were entirely left to our own judgment. I found
on the other fide many that were well inclined,
though they were quite inactive. Thefe and
other reflections induced me to think, that virtue confifted in nothing elfe, but in actions
which are ufeful to fociety, and in a defire of
producing them.—Ambition, love of our native
country, natural inclination to what is good, a
well regulated felf-love, or even the knowledge
of religion, when they are confidered as motives
of virtue, I looked upon as indifferent things,
according as they happened to make different
impreffions upon particular perfons.—Reafon
and reflection were, in my opinion, the
only teachers and regulators of virtue. He is
to be counted the moft virtuous whofe actions
are the moft ufeful, the moft difficult to be
practifed, and of the moft extenfive influence;

and

and no one could be blamed who obferved the laws of his country, and the true principles of honour.

I thought I had found in the nature of man fufficient powers and fprings to make him virtuous. Revealed religion I looked upon as unneceffary, fince it could only convince men, whofe underftandings were lefs enlightened, of the obligations of virtue. The effects of religion I never had perceived within me, at leaft I never had regarded them. Its doctrines feemed to contradict all the reft of my notions. Its morals appeared to me too fevere, and I believed I found them full as clear, perfect and ufeful in the writings of philofophers. If you add to this, the following doubts: Religion is known but among a fmall part of mankind,—it makes very little impreffion upon the mind,—its abufe has produced a great many fatal confequences,—few of thofe that know it, act agreeably to its precepts,—but very little hope there is of a future life,—God's mercy will forgive the faults of error and precipitation,—the nature of man contradicts the precepts of religion and oppofes them :—and you will eafily imagine what inferences I drew from thence.

Reafon

Reason guided by underſtanding, ſupported by ambition, ſelf-love, and a natural inclination to what is good, became now the principles which determined my actions. To how many errors and miſtakes was I expoſed! I found it not difficult to excuſe my favourite paſſions, and give myſelf up entirely to the gratification of them. The indulgence of my ſenſual deſires appeared to me, at the moſt, to be only weakneſs, if they were not attended with bad conſequences either to myſelf or to others, and this could be prevented by prudence and circumſpection. I found that many who pretended to honour and virtue, yet indulged them, and excuſed them. The manners of the times permitted ſilently liberties which were condemned only by the too rigid moraliſt, but were treated with more indulgence and tenderneſs by thoſe, that are acquainted with the human heart. Continence was in my eyes a virtue produced by prejudice. Whole nations ſubſiſted without knowing or practiſing this virtue.

It is very humiliating to me, my dear friend, to repeat to you theſe falſe excuſes, which appear to me at preſent highly abſurd. However, they will be found adopted by all thoſe, that act not quite thoughtleſly, but attempt to apologize

by

by arguments for the irregularity of their life. How eafy is it in this manner to palliate and to juftify the indulgence of every one of our paffions ? The ambitious man finds in all that he does patriotifm and a laudable ambition; the felf-conceited a noble pride, founded upon merit, and a juftice which he owes to himfelf; the flanderer a love of truth, and innocent mirth, &c.

I hoped to efcape thofe errors by an accurate felf-examination, and an enquiry into the confequences of my actions. But how was I able to do this, were it poffible to anfwer only for their moft immediate confequences ? Did I not deceive myfelf, in believing that I had the ftrongeft intentions of doing good, and did really as much as I was able to do ? Was it infatuation, infenfibility and affectation, when I flattered myfelf to find, firmnefs and tranquillity in my prefent misfortunes ? When I fearched into the caufes of them, I confidered only the political ones, and how much could I find to excufe myfelf, if I did but confider the nature of my fituation, and the accidents it was fubject to ? I had but a confufed idea of my moral principles, and I could not reject them, without depriving myfelf of all comfort. My expectations of futurity I before told you: and

by

by diffipating my thoughts and directing them to other fubjects, I could more eafily bear my misfortunes, and fupport my natural difpofition, as the impreffion, an object makes upon our mind, grows ftronger by conftantly reflecting upon it.

In this condition, my dear friend, you found me, and we began our Conferences. You remember how much I thought myfelf convinced of my principles, how ftrongly they were imprinted on my mind, and how much I guarded againft every paffion that could rife within me. However, I found it but juft to enquire into a matter that concerned my happinefs, and which might be of fuch confequence with regard to futurity. An opinion, where the greateft probability amounts to certainty, receives ftill greater by examining that which is oppofite to it. And to anfwer the objections which can be made againft it, requires at leaft as much attention from us, as we beftowed upon the examination of the arguments which induced us to embrace it.

Upon confidering my moral principles, I began immediately to doubt, whether they might not have been the caufe of my miftaking what I

chiefly

chiefly aimed at, namely, the inward satisfaction
of my actions. I was very sensible, how much
I deserved the reproaches of my own mind
as well as those of others, if it was only on account of my unhappy friends, whose misfortunes
greatly affected me. Might it not have been
better, to have judged of my actions more by
thinking from whence they arose, than to what
they related, and what their consequences were?
How few would my pleasures have been, and
how little would my life have been! However,
I should now have less necessity for repentance
and contrition, though before I must have had
greater conflicts and struggles with myself. The
times of my suffering are only altered. If the
first had taken place, my troubles would have
been shorter, but now I feel an uniform and
continued series of disagreeable sensations. I
then should have suffered only myself.—And
what satisfaction have I received of all which fortune seemed to promise me? My passions were
perhaps gratified, but in such a manner as always left a void after them. My wishes were
satisfied, but the anxiety I was under to preserve
my possessions, took away the greatest part of
their pleasure. I enjoyed a variety of pleasures,
which by their nature destroy one another, and
are at the most nothing more than dissipations.

2

I grew

I grew at laſt inſenſible to the pleaſures of life, which is the natural conſequence of being in poſſeſſion of every thing which can render life eaſy and agreeable. I did not enjoy the comforts of friendſhip and ſociety, as the ſituation I was in was extremely diſſipated, and it required attention to a hundred trifles; beſides, the impoſſibility of diverting my thoughts from the little dependance I could place on it, would not admit of any real ſatisfaction. Suppoſing too, that I even had good intentions, and the lawful means of putting them into practice, and that my faults were only the conſequences of inattention and natural weakneſs, I ſhould loſe all the comforts I might derive from the former, by reproaching myſelf on account of the latter. I might have avoided them, by recollecting all their conſequences, according to their different relations. However, even this was impoſſible when my paſſions repreſented to me the danger my own happineſs and that of others was in, and the impoſſibility of providing againſt conſequences which were then at a diſtance. When my paſſions and my reaſon were in oppoſition, and the underſtanding was to decide, I might have been always inclined in favour of that ſide where the pleaſure ſeemed neareſt, and

pain

pain at the greateſt diſtance. Ambition and ſelf-love, and the influence our actions have upon one another are eaſily explained, and in their application, found ſufficient to anſwer their purpoſes. I could not now deny but that my principles were not capable of procuring me moral tranquillity, that my paſſions had been the chief ſprings of all my actions, and that no other comfort remained for me, but that which is derived from the inconſtancy of human affairs. I might be indebted to my principles for my ſucceſs in life, and my activity: but I muſt reject them, if they induced me to commit an action which deſerves reproaches, and which deſtroys my inward happineſs.

I was ready to give up my former principles as ſoon as I could diſcover better. I ſaw that they were liable to two objections. My way of judging of the morality of my actions from their relations and conſequences, was neither ſafe nor certain. My arguments in favour of virtue, might be equally applicable to juſtify the gratification of my paſſions, as to controul them. They were not ſufficiently ſtrong in their effects, and were alſo liable to be miſinterpreted, when my paſſions became too impetuous. Conſcience, the inward ſenſe of

what

what is good or bad, and the fear of God, feemed not to obviate this difficulty. I found fufficient, reafons to difallow them, and my fenfuality would not permit me to feel their impreffion. Should thefe have taught me how to act with propriety and juftice in all circumftances, and to make myfelf eafy, though the confequences, the opinion of men, and the reproaches of my friends had been againft me? No doubt. But then my actions fhould have been derived from my fentiments, and thefe fhould have had a certain fixed rule to direct them, to prevent me from falling into error.

I perceived my miftake, that I had placed virtue in actions only, without regard to their intentions, and by this I had loft what I was perfuing, inward contentment. *Gellert* fhewed me the means by which I might have avoided it. *Jerufalem* convinced me what ftrength and affiftance true devotion furnifhes us with. *Reimarus* removed the doubts I had, that God did not concern himfelf with the moral actions of men. I will not repeat the feries of meditations, which convinced me of the truth of what thefe excellent writers teach us. I fhall only repeat a

few

few of them, and thofe only which made the ſtrongeſt impreſſion upon me.

Was it not the love of ſenſual pleaſures, which made me deny that truth, which my reaſon aſſented to, and repreſented other objects and falſe notions as matters of conſequence?—Is there more ſafety and wiſdom, where I find ſimple principles, which may be practiſed with clearneſs in all caſes without exception, or there, where the variety of opinions, and the conditions which are innumerable, require more time for enquiring than action? If the moral diſtinction between virtue and vice, is not to be founded on the intentions, none can pretend to virtue, at leaſt, it does not depend upon our own will. The prudent, the cautious, the crafty, the hypocrite ſhall then be virtuous; the ſimple, the careleſs, the unhappy, the ſincere ſhall then be called wicked. My inward ſatisfaction will depend on the opinion of others and on accidents, if I cannot judge of my intentions by ſome fixed rules.

It is a very narrow notion to think that the univerſe taken together, is only worth the attention of the ſupreme Being. We know that

knowledge

knowledge and a combination of many particular events and operating caufes, which all tend
to one end, produce actions of the greateft moral
confequence to fociety. It is beyond man's
capacity to reprefent to his mind thefe things at
once. He lofes the fight of the whole, by examining the parts feparately. He is therefore
obliged to fix his attention only upon thofe
caufes which are neareft and moft fenfible in
their effects. Thofe which are more remote
he muft leave to chance, or which is the fame
thing, he muft fuppofe, that they will not fail of
their end, though they are not in his power.
But let us go further. He that views the moft
remote poffible event at one view, and knows
how to direct every one of them to anfwer his
particular defign, and to remove with the
greateft facility the obftacles which are in his
way, deferves undoubtedly the name of a
great man. The more regularity and harmony
he can give to every part, the more can he depend upon the event. It muft be difpleafing, if
he cannot effect this. The faults of fingle fol-
diers cannot be pleafing to a good general in
time of action if he perceives them, and he needs
muft difcover them. Many little irregularities
render the whole imperfect. We overlook
them, becaufe our abilities will not permit us to

do

do otherwife, and we are ufed to defpife what we cannot attain to for want of power. But it is abfurd to apply this manner of reafoning to God, and to believe that he follows our example, and takes care of the whole without attending to particular imperfections. That pofition : God has regulated the whole in fuch a manner, that the particular irregularities of men are of no confequence, and therefore indifferent to him, is founded upon this principle; that man acts always according to a fatal neceffity. God therefore will certainly obferve, how far every individual acts by his free-will confiftently with his determination. Univerfal happinefs cannot take place unlefs every one contributes towards it.

It is no argument, that God has difpenfed fuch a number of good things in nature, and the inftincts of man are fo various, that every one may be happy. Others generally fuffer and are made uneafy when our poffeffions encreafe, and our enjoyments are great. Therefore the defire of encreafing our happinefs in this manner, is inconfiftent with our determination. The increafe of our moral perfections can take place without detriment and for the benefit of the whole. The fmalleft tranfgreffion in this refpect

muft

muſt be diſpleaſing to God. What apologies can we make ? Perhaps ſuch as a courtier makes when he deceives his maſter to ſerve his friend, or a miniſter of ſtate when he loſes ſight of the public good to ſerve his own private in‑tereſt.

It is owing to pride and prejudice in favour of our own internal ſtrength, when we hope to be virtuous through our own powers. We commonly perceive in objects before us what we want to ſee. It is impoſſible to have all thoſe ideas preſent in our mind which are required to draw juſt concluſions. We find thoſe ſooneſt which anſwer our purpoſes. The cool philoſopher finds frequently that to be falſe, which he took for granted before he begun his inquiries. And ſince all this is moſt certain, how eaſy muſt it be for us to convince ourſelves, how uncertain our way of reaſoning is, when it concerns things which we earneſtly deſire, and when the queſtion is, whether we ſhall allow or refuſe ourſelves the enjoyment of them. A lively impreſſion, which preſents us with the arguments on both ſides, is the only means to keep us from error.

Q						How

How many difagreeable moments did thefe reflexions caufe me! They were fufficient to convince me how much I had erred from what I was ftriving for; how little I had acted according to the true end of my nature, and how much I was to blame. I felt with pain, that I had followed falfe principles and narrow prejudices. You know, how much I was concerned for the misfortune of thofe perfons with whom I had been connected. Nothing was now left me, but to endeavour to leffen the uneafinefs I felt, fince I found myfelf the only caufe of it. But my pain became more violent, whenever I confidered my fituation from that fide, where it made the greateft impreffion upon me. The many confequences of my vices, and the thoughts that I had offended God, moft deeply affected me.

However, my former turn of thought made me miftruft, whether my prefent fentiments were not perhaps more a confequence of my prefent fituation of mind, than of the conviction of my underftanding. The uncertainty I was under concerning the nature of my foul and its immortality, prevented me from giving my full affent. *Bonnet* anfwered all my doubts as far as mere reafon can arrive at any certainty. I could

not

not deny that my prefent difpofition of mind, if I compared it with a former one, was better adapted to enquire after truth and to find it out. Before, I ufed to pafs over every thing which oppofed my paffions, and found good what they defired: but I was now more inclined to be cautious and miftruftful, and it is a great thing to acknowledge our faults. The more I confidered my former doubts, the lefs reafon I had to think them to be of any confequence. I examined every particular argument in favour of my former opinion: but at laft I was obliged to own with *Gellert*, that if all that we know from reafon, of God, of our foul, and our moral happinefs was uncertain, truth muft be folly, and error muft be wifdom.

You know, my dear friend, how much thefe truths increafed my uneafinefs: I faw continually new objects, which hitherto had remained undifcovered, on account of the livelinefs of the firft impreffions. The indifference I had to any fixed principles, my neglect of every fingle obligation, my remiffnefs in doing good, when I had opportunity or abilities for it, the mifchief which my example, and the propagating of my principles might do, the difpleafure of God which my tranfgreffions muft draw upon me; all thefe circumftances

cumftances united produced in me the greateft anxiety. And how could I leffen the anxiety fuch reflexions occafioned me ? I took the refolution to act according to that truth which I had found. I had a lively fenfe of my former tranfgreffions, but from whence could I derive the hopes of repairing what was done, or burying it in oblivion ? It is uncertain whether good intentions will always be equally ftrong ; perhaps new inticements and the errors of my underftanding may overpower them. The thought which is directed towards God, the fentiments, confcience, and the recollection of its reproaches can be weakened. Virtue cannot prevent vice from being hurtful, much lefs can it repair the damage which is done. Time, opportunities and former fituations were loft to me, and but little comfort was left me from this view. When I reflected on the idea which reafon afforded me of God, I had but little hopes to flatter myfelf that my fins would be forgiven. If I attempted to form the moft favourable idea of God's mercy, that he would confider the weaknefs and imperfection of human nature, I faw at the fame time his juftice and immutability, which were directly contrary to this idea. The confequences of actions happen in the moral world as they do in the natural, according to certain fixed rules. To thefe fettled laws God leaves the fate of man,

and

and his fate depends upon himself, since he acts with liberty. Experience teaches us sufficiently that no exception is to be made to this rule. Every crime and every transgression carries its punishment along with it. Perhaps no instance can be produced which would not convince us of the truth of this assertion, if we estimate man's happiness according to what he feels within himself, and not according to the general notions we have of good fortune. The irregularity and variety of our passions are evils, and the painful consciousness of the crimes we have committed never leaves us. Will God produce good out of evil, to remove the misfortunes which our sins brought upon us, and which are a proof of his displeasure?

Of these truths I always have been convinced, but I looked upon them as necessary evils connected with our fate, which would cease with this life, even if they could be called a kind of punishment. I could diminish the lively impression of these evils by a firmness of soul, by coolness of mind acquired by practice, and a contemplation of the evils themselves, without fancying them greater than they really are. Patience, I fancied, might make us indifferent about them, and dissipation make us entirely forget them.

Sup-

Supported by thefe confiderations, I fubmitted to my misfortunes, fince I could not avoid them, and they appeared to me in this light lefs terrible. We are apt to fuppofe an old erroneous tenet to be true, as we are apt to believe an often repeated falfhood. That hope which makes death the end of all our misfortunes, requires the greateft firmnefs and indifference to fupport it. You know thofe reafons which ferve to infpire us with comfort in regard to a future life, agreeably to my former principles, and confidering eternity in the view I did. However, the uncertainty of all this would have occafioned the greateft uneafinefs, even at a time when I fhould not have been diffident of my own ftrength.

The continuation of my moral enquiries did not decreafe this. Remembrance will be an effential matter, whereby my future ftate is to be connected with my prefent one. How fhould I obliterate the memory of thefe reproaches which torment me now? how fhould I regulate my fentiments? Every thing renewed the confcioufnefs of my former reproaches, and I was fo accuftomed to my way of thinking, that it would, perhaps, be ftill more difficult to leave it, than any other cuftom I have been ufed to. I found this to be the fact; for my underftanding,

though

though convinced, yet thought, doubted, apologized, and faw a poffibility of my not being in the wrong. The repeating of thofe reflexions which had fhewn me my errors, brought me back to truth: however, I could not arrive at any certainty in regard to a future life, and the confequences of my tranfgreffions with refpect to the Deity. The truths of revealed religion did not yet make any impreffion upon my mind.

You gave me the Hiftory of the three laft Years of the Life of Chrift ; I read it, and how excellent did I find the doctrines it contained ! Its moral principles are fimple, clear, and adapted to every fituation in life. Whoever knows how difficult it is to reduce a fcience to general principles, cannot obferve this without furprize, even if he confiders Chrift only as a mere man. I was afhamed to find here again what I formerly had forgot, and afterwards believed it to be owing to feveral books of morality I had read. I was convinced that the fpirit of revenge was wrong, but I did not remember that Chrift had ever forbid it. The love of our enemies had never before been taught us, and it appeared to me contradictory to our nature. I wifhed to be convinced, not only of this chriftian duty, but

of

of all the other principles of Chrift's doctrine.
Thofe objections which were made againft Chrift
on account of his birth, his education in Egypt,
and the inftruction he received in the fciences
which were taught by the Jews, made me imagine that his doctrine was more than human.
How could he be above the prejudices of education and inftruction ? how could he teach things
quite contrary to them ? There is nothing contradictory in his doctrines or in his actions. We can
eafily convince ourfelves of this, if we only avoid
judging according to our own manners, cuftoms
and prejudices.   Not to get acquainted with the
Gofpel becaufe Chrift was a Jew, is the fame in
reality as if one fhould object to read the writings
of Mendelfon *, becaufe he is a Jew.   The life
of Chrift, publifhed at Zurich, delivers the hiftory in a modern ftile, and in an uninterrupted
connexion.   Though the manner of writing, and
the expreffions ufed by the facred penmen, were
not fuch as I greatly objected to, yet they have
prevented me from reading ferious enquiries on
the facred writings, fince I ufed to read moftly
thofe books which were written againft them.

* Mofes Mendelfon is a learned Jew, now living at
Berlin.   He has acquired great reputation by his philofophical writings.   Some mention is made of him in the Critical Review, vol. xxxiv. p. 223.

A divine

A divine revelation had appeared to me unneceſſary, its hiſtorical evidence dubious, and the
facts related ſeemed to be very improbable. I
now began to be convinced of the neceſſity of a
divine revelation ; for many reaſons, and in particular the neceſſity of finding out ſtronger motives
for virtue than thoſe which reaſon only, ſupply us
with, would no longer let me doubt of it.
Bonnet and *Leſs* proved to me the poſſibility and
credibility of the miracles. *Weſt* might have
been fully ſufficient to have convinced me of the
truth of Chriſt's reſurrection, but you know I
examined all the reſt of the arguments. I believed many facts which are taught in natural
philoſophy, where I could not diſcover the cauſe
and its effects ; why did I doubt of the poſſibility of miracles, when the deſign intended by
them is ſo clear ? Certainly there was no other
reaſon, but becauſe I was not inclined to it. I am
now as ſure of the facts the truth of a divine revelation is founded upon, as if I ſaw them before
me. When a number of credible witneſſes agree
in things in which our ſenſes are only concerned,
I am as much convinced of them, as if I knew
them from my own experience. It was neceſſary
for me to attain the higheſt degree of certainty in
this reſpect, in order to remove all doubts which
now and then perplexed my underſtanding ; and

I praiſe

I praise God, with a lively sense of gratitude, that I have met with success.

You know, my dear friend, with what a disposition of heart I began these enquiries. My former principles taught me to guard against every violent affection. Use, the nature of my employments, and the manner in which I rose to my former prosperity, had procured me a habit of acting in all circumstances with coolness. I found I had reason to be apprehensive, that in one point tenderness would get the better of my understanding, and this was friendship. This only made me sensible of the situation I was in; for neither the possession nor the loss of my former prosperity affected me much. I was always upon my guard against my fancy, and for this very reason I avoided reading poets and other authors that could inflame it. I was often doubtful about my opinions and mistrusted them, but when I once had adopted them as true, I avoided further enquiry and change, because they prevented my putting them in practice. My obstinacy, and my indefatigable pursuit of the same object, together with the coolness I acted with, have contributed much to my prosperity and my misfortune, and they might have been the cause of making me lose everlasting happiness, if the

many

many proofs which I have heard and read of it, had not recovered me from my error.

The examination of the historical arguments of divine revelation with care and precaution, has satisfied and convinced me. Being certain of this, it was an easy matter for me to remove all my other doubts. I was certain there must be stronger arguments to convince us, than those which mere reason furnishes us with. A proper degree of self-love, honour, and love of virtue, are liable to so many explanations, our understanding can so easily be imposed upon, and our will is with so much difficulty restrained, from considering the object only from the point of view in which it is most agreeable. Nothing can have greater effect upon our conduct than a habit of devotion, and though I thought religion always useful for this purpose, I nevertheless believed, that a sufficient knowledge of our duty, and a desire of acting conformably to it, were at all times sufficient motives for being virtuous.

I found the origin of religious ceremonies in the natural fears and infirmities of men; I saw how much the many revolutions which have happened, have increased them, and what influence the manners, customs, and ways of thinking of nations had had upon them.
This

This confideration made me acknowledge with gratitude, the excellence of chriftianity, whofe ceremonies are fo clear and well founded. We accuftom ourfelves to thofe things which we fee daily; we perceive how they happen, but are unacquainted with their remote caufes, which, at laft, lofe all their effect. For this very reafon the idea of the exiftence of a God, and his providence over all things, is fo little difcoverable in our actions. Our internal fenfations, confcience, and the contemplation of nature, feldom carry us fo far back as to make any alteration in our moral conduct. The will of God, in regard to our happinefs, remains doubtful to our reafon, as long as it is left to the decifion of our underftanding. The various revelations in the Old Teftament, prophecies, laws, and remarkable punifhments, could be looked upon as impoftures of men, and as things which arofe from natural caufes: but fince Chrift has come into the world, and told us that his doctrine was the will of God, and that he was fent to inftruct us, and that he himfelf was the true God; no further excufe remains for our ignorance and error. Every one to whom the opportunity is offered, and who will accept of it, can eafily convince himfelf of its truth.

An

(237)

An unexceptionable evidence is as certain as
our own experience, and whoever wants the latter
teltimony, may confider the prefent ftate of the
Jews, who are living witneffes of the truth of
Chrift's prophecies. No perfecution, oppref-
fion and contempt could ever induce this people
to mix with other nations, and to adopt their
manners and cuftoms. The wonders by which
Chrift has confirmed his divine miffion can be
proved wi.h the fame certainty. They were
performed without any preparations, without
any circumftances that might have impofed upon
the fenfes, without any previous expectation, before a number of incredulous fpectators, in fuch a
manner that no impofition can poffibly be fuf-
pected. They were befides of fuch a nature that
every man of common underftanding might perceive, that thofe means which were made ufe of
never could produce fuch effects. A man, born
blind, recovered his fight; one that had lain
four days in the grave, came to life again; a pa-
ralytic was reftored to health again;—and all this
by only fpeaking a word. If we were to fuppofe that in the regular courfe of nature fuch a
thing was to happen juft at this time, or that God
produced thefe events by the interpofition of
almighty power, it follows, in the firft inftance,
that Chrift muft have been informed of it before;

                                    and,

and, in the second, that God heard him. Both which are equally a miracle, and a proof of his divine miffion.

As foon as I was convinced of this; nothing remained, but to examine whether the doctrine which he preached, and we are to believe, contained any thing that contradicted reafon. He wifhes me to be happy and to be virtuous; to feek for my happinefs not in fenfual pleafures and in the gratification of my paffions; to love God above all things, and to deal with my neighbour as I wifh to be dealt with myfelf. He enjoins me to believe that there is another life after this, where the condition I fhall be in will depend on the fentiments and actions of this prefent life; that without the affiftance of God I am unable either to think or act virtuoufly; that God will do nothing extraordinary for me, to remove the fatal confequences of my tranfgreffions, which I have to fear in a future life; that God has fent him to give me the moft undoubted affurance of his juftice, and his immutability: but that this, at the fame time, is the greateft proof of his love towards me, fince through him I am made acquainted with the fureft way of becoming acceptable to the Supreme Being.—All this is very confiftent with reafon.

But

But Chrift commanded me befides, to believe that he was very God and very man, and the fon of God; and that in the divine nature the Father, Son and Holy Ghoft are one. This feemed to contradict all my notions which I hitherto had entertained. But I knew that the word of Chrift was always truth, that he muft be fully acquainted with thefe myfteries, and that I had not the leaft reafon to imagine, he would require of me to believe any thing that was contradictory to reafon. It might be above my underftanding; but how many things do we meet with in the courfe of nature, whofe exiftence we cannot deny, without being able to explain why they are fo, and how they are connected with their caufes? I thought myfelf obliged to believe thefe myfteries upon the word of Chrift; neverthelelefs I confidered them with great attention, without finding them contradictory. God might reveal himfelf unto us in a different manner from that he had hitherto made ufe of, though our reafon was unable to explain it. God chofe for this the language of men, and thofe figns by which we communicate our ideas to each other. The very God who fpoke through Chrift, was the fame who made himfelf known to us as Father and Holy Ghoft. It cannot be denied that God, when we confider his nature as well as his attributes, could

not

not be able to produce various effects at the same time, without our being obliged to believe that his essence is divided. It therefore was the Supreme Being, which reason teaches us to be one, that operated through Christ, though it only appeared under a human form, and made itself known to us, since we ourselves could not perceive it by our senses. We are used to apply more common notions to less known objects, in order to explain more exactly the idea we have of them. This has recalled to my mind the idea of gravity, which in different bodies operates differently, though the power itself is always the same. I have not found any thing contradictory in this idea of the Trinity, notwithstanding that I have reflected upon this subject with great accuracy, and in more different views than I have done here. In the same manner I have found nothing contradictory in Christ's making known unto us God as Father and Holy Ghost.

How easily can we fall into errors if any one wants to give us an idea of a thing unknown to us, by comparing it with another we are acquainted with. I dare not apply, in such cases, every little idea annexed to the object, to the other which I want to explain it by. If I was to tell an Indian, that the water in our climate grows

grows fometimes as hard as ftone, and he fhould then think that ice might be made red hot, and be ufed for materials to build a houfe, he would think fomething very abfurd. Chrift has fhewn us God under the character of a **Father**, in order to compare his love towards his fon under a figure that was known to us. A philofophical defcription would not have cleared it up better. But if we were to apply to God every thing that falls under the notion of a father, we fhould be liable to the fame miftake of the Indian. In the fame manner we can conceive how Chrift, the Son of God, was born from his Father. From all eternity God would make himfelf known to us by Chrift, and the word, *beget*, conveyed to us the beft idea of this myfterious tranfaction within the Deity. We can likewife form an idea of that relation which fubfifts between the Father and Chrift, by thinking him the Son of God; we are only to feparate thofe ideas which reafon teaches us not to be applicable to God. The Son has his effence of the Father, and it is the fame with that the Father has; he loves him, and what is his is likewife the Son's.

Laftly, Chrift promifes, that after his departure, the fpirit of God fhould confirm thefe truths which he had taught. This was done in

R a vifible

a vifible manner by thofe gifts which the Apoftles received, and he continues to operate upon thofe who obferve the doctrines of Chrift, and, by fo doing, are capable of making good refolutions, and of thinking and of acting as it pleafes God.

God has now revealed himfelf in a threefold manner, and every one of them reprefents him to me as the author and promoter of my happinefs. We are ufed to exprefs compound ideas with a fingle word, to avoid prolixity. For this reafon, the word, perfon, was made ufe of in the doctrine of the Trinity. If I now find a con-tradiction, when I fay, " There is one God, but three perfons in him," the fault is then in my underftanding; its notions are not juft, it com-bines the common notions of God and of a per-fon in a ftrange and improper manner. If I was to oppofe the doctrine of the Trinity, I fhould act like the Indian who would not believe the exift-ence of ice, becaufe he was told that it would melt and turn into water again in the fummer and by the fire.

I reflect on Chrift's redemption, to which my underftanding has no objection. I am convinced how neceffary it is for my happinefs to know, that my actions are not indifferent to God: and now I am affured, with all hiftorical certainty, that
Chrift

Chrift lived, and was proved to be intimately connected with the Deity, by performing fuch actions as cannot be explained by natural caufes. He affures me of his friendfhip, and I cannot conceive what advantage could arife to him, or what intention he could have to deceive me. I am inclined to believe my friend in a matter, where his former tranfactions have convinced me that his knowledge is fuperior to mine, if my underftanding finds nothing contradictory in it. Chrift tells me, that he knows the will of God, and that God himfelf fpeaks to me through him, which certainly is the beft way to learn his will. The doctrines he inculcates agree with thofe which my own reafon teaches to be neceffary for my happinefs; and I was fenfible how eafily I could mifapply thefe doctrines, if I did not always remember, that God faw my actions. Whatever determined me formerly to act in fuch a manner as my own happinefs required, I owed to other caufes and intentions, and why fhould I not have interpreted the actions and kindnefs of Chrift in the fame manner? He recalls to my memory whatever I know from political and natural hiftory, and exprefly affures me that extraordinary events were defigned for this purpofe. He fums up all thefe together in this fingle propofition: God loves man as a father. Now God

R 2

fhews

fhews himfelf as a friend. Chrift is defpifed and looked upon as an impoftor, though he teaches nothing but the manner in which we may become happy, and performs actions which are beneficial to men. To convince me more fully of his fincerity, he gives me the greateft proof of his friendfhip : he fuffers death in confirmation of a truth, of which was I not certain, and did not confirm it accordingly, I could not be happy. God, with whom Chrift is clofely connected, permits all this. Can I now ever doubt that God's providence extends to me ? I know from reafon that the regularity in my conduct muft be pleafing to God, and that it is impoffible for me to act agreeably to it, if I had not a lively idea of God's omniprefence. I know him now in the character of father and friend, and under both thefe denominations always fhall reprefent him to me.

Chrift enjoins me in particular to believe in him, and to remember his love towards me, and really without this I fhould not be able to perform my duty. The more I reflect on thefe truths which he has taught me, the more I find how far I am from living in a manner that would pleafe God. Should I not be extremely forry for having offended a friend whom I neglected,

and

and would not know ? I was uncertain whether there might be a future life, and whether the confequences of my offences could have any influence upon it. Chrift promifes me, that God will avert thefe evils, if I place an unreferved confidence in his friendfhip.—I am eafy with regard to what is paffed, however I know how foon a prefent idea effaces a former one : and this is the cafe when I ftrongly defire what I fhould deny myfelf. The doctrine of Chrift informs me of this likewife. The fpirit of God will revive thefe doctrines within me, if I make myfelf well acquainted with them, and conftantly endeavour to put them into practice.

There is nothing in my reafon that could prevent me from being fully convinced, that thefe means Chrift teaches me, are the only ones that can render me virtuous and acceptable to God. It is my own fault if I do not receive and make ufe of them ; for I then refufe to be happy. God will not, for my own fake, interrupt thofe regulations he has made in regard to future life. I muft feel the bad confequences of my neglect, and of the vain hopes which I placed in God's mercy. I am obliged to him that he has made himfelf known to me in fo extraordinary a manner. I could not even expect to deferve the

happy

happy confequences of the refolution I had made of obeying Chrift's precepts; fince, without the perpetual affiftance of the Spirit of God, I am unable to obey them, and fince, notwithftanding this affiftance, I fo frequently neglect and forget them.

This is entirely confiftent with the doctrine of Chrift. I always-believe thefe three but one God, and the idea I have makes the Trinity not different Deities. All this is conformable with my reafon. However, I durft not hope, confidering God and myfelf, that this Supreme Being would be fo merciful as to teach me how, according to the fentiments of my own underftanding, I could be happy. Full of gratitude and confcious of my being unworthy, I adore it, and fhall never defift to adore and praife the mercy, fhewn to me through Chrift.

I was greatly affected when I read the life of Chrift. It increafed my pains, and gave me new ones. But I was afraid it was owing to my difpofition of mind, becaufe I was ftill full of doubts. The examination of the truth of the chriftian religion became more agreeable to me, the more I advanced in it. My reafon was fatisfied with it, but I did not find thofe inward
feelings,

feelings, which, as I had heard, were connected with true chriftianity, according to the
confufed notions of fome people. *Spalding's*
book fet me right in this point. I found here
how difficult it is to get rid of opinions and
fentiments which are become a fecond nature,
though I was convinced that they were falfe and
deftructive. My doubts arofe contrary to my
wifhes, and I did not pafs them over before I
had examined them feparately, and had frequently reflected on the arguments for the truth
of religion.

The application of its doctrines produced within me a lively repentance, forrow, fhame, and
fentiments of humility. Without anxiety or
fear I expected the comfort which the Gofpel
promifed me. To regulate my fentiments agreeable to its precepts, was my chief employment.
The perpetual remembrance of the greatnefs of
God's mercy, which was fhewn to me by the
redemption of Chrift, made me overcome thofe
difficulties I found arofe from my natural difpofition. The pleafure of finding a happinefs,
which I hitherto had wilfully renounced,
could not produce in me a lively joy, becaufe
I remembered that I had been feeking it formerly
in a manner that could not pleafe God. It was

impoffible

impoffible to make myfelf perfectly eafy. I was prevented from this, by the thought that if I had formerly entertained my prefent fentiments, I might have thereby excited thofe perfons, with whom I had been moft intimate, to enquire after the fame happinefs. Now I am praying to God that he may do it, and I am perfuaded he will, fince Chrift has promifed it. Prayer takes away the uneafinefs I have on this and other points, which are difagreeable for me to remember. I direct my thoughts to God, repeat the doctrines of the Gofpel, reflect on their connexion, apply them to myfelf, and if I addrefs myfelf to God in prayer in the name of my Redeemer for thefe mercies, I find that thefe contribute to render me eafy, and I admire with gratitude the power of religion.

I fee now how little a chriftian deferves the reproach of being felf-interefted. He prays, and receives no reward, but by endeavouring to pleafe God, when he regulates his fentiments according to his precepts. If God hears him, he acknowledges with gratitude, that the doctrine of Chrift procured him the means for it, he remembers his own weaknefs and praifes the affiftance of God. No blind confidence in God's mercy, nor the hope of the happinefs of a future life," inflame his imagination, which regulates itself after the difposition the mind is in. *Bonnet* and *Lavater* conducted me gradually to hopeful profpects of eternity, but I rather perufe the writings of *Spalding*, *Alberti*, and others of this kind.

The remembrance how indefatigable I had been for many years together, in collecting and practifing my former principles, obliged me to keep a watchful eye over myfelf, for fear they might infenfibly have an influence upon my new fentiments. How earneftly do l wifh to efface the impreffion which I have made upon others. I never intended to propagate my principles, though I never denied them. I have reafon to lament a crime, which I muft be afhamed to own even before a world that thinks as I did formerly ; and I feel on this account, a more lively fenfe of thofe tranfgreffions which I have committed againft God. My fenfe of friendfhip and humanity always recalls to my mind the bad example, and the feduction by which I have contributed to make others look upon fenfual pleafures as the chief end of our exiftence. Nothing that relates to my prefent fituation difturbs me, except this and other reflections of this kind. To terror and a fear that deprives us of the ufe of reafon, I always

I always have been almoſt a ſtranger. Death was not terrible to me, ſince I looked upon it as a conſequence of natural cauſes, and a fate that is unavoidable. At preſent nothing appears dreadful to me, ſince I know that I depend upon God, and am convinced of the truth of religion, and expect a happy eternity.

I praiſe God ſincerely, that I arrived at this conviction, and I acknowledge it with a lively ſenſe of gratitude, that you, my dear friend, have conducted me to it. You choſe the only method which ſuits the diſpoſition of my mind. Rhetorical figures and declamations would have had but little effect upon me. Suppoſe you had endeavoured to enflame my imagination and paſſions, my principles would ſoon have compoſed them again. The doctrines of religion I always remembered; for in the earlier days of my life I had frequently read the Bible, though with ideas quite different from thoſe I entertain at preſent. Scripture expreſſions were familiar to me, and I afterwards had contracted habits to connect them with all the doubts and opinions which correſponded with my principles. Before my underſtanding was convinced that they were falſe, you could not expect that I ſhould ſincerely believe the truth of revelation. I ſoon
diſcovered

difcovered my tranfgreffion of moral duties; but you know, and I have told you how much felf-denial it coft me, to acknowledge my errors. My pride would fain animate me to conquer the fear of eternity like any other fear. My defire of being as happy in this world as poffible, had taught me to defpife every kind of danger, and this arofe more from a cool reflection on the latter, than from a lively fenfe of happinefs. Truth only could bring me back, and you left me to my own refearches to difcover it. You pro-pofed to me, only thofe confequences which my turn of thought and actions could have in regard to fuch of my friends, as were concerned in my fate as well as I was in theirs. I was on this account always much affected, and this alone could put my mind in agitation. However, it could not have difpofed me to embrace religion, if I had not clearly feen its truth; and I am convinced I fhould have em-braced it before this time, if its evidence had ever been laid before me, and taught me in the manner you did. I found in religion what I wifhed for, and what I thought I durft not hope for. I knew its truths only under certain images and expreffions, to which I at laft familiarized myfelf fo much, that I forgot to combine any ideas with them. The firft inftruction can

I   be be effected only by sensible representations, but I used them afterwards for raising doubts against religion; and this prevented me from expecting those comforts from it which I sought for.

I had two reasons for not examining more minutely the arguments for religion. You know the objections commonly made against the credibility of supernatural events and miracles. I was not acquainted with *Less* and *Bonnet*, and the objections appeared to me unanswerable. When on the other hand I reflected on the redemption of Christ, it seemed to contradict all my notions. To shew to man the love and justice of God in a stronger light, redemption is commonly represented thus: That God was angry on account of the sins of men, but loved them to such a degree that he was desirous of pardoning them. But this could not be effected without the death of his only begotten Son, who is God himself. The notions which I had of God, excited on this point particularly my attention, and it seemed hard to me to reconcile the necessity of redemption with them. I asked: Cannot God forgive without this! I was puzzled·when I considered redemption only in relation to God. But as soon as you taught me to reflect on it, in relation to man, you removed all my doubts, I

found

found the neceſſity and the greatneſs of God's mercy in giving his own Son to make men happy.

As to practical chriſtianity, it always has offended me to find ſo many whoſe ſentiments and actions ſo little correſponded to their pretended faith, and ſenſe of truth. I diſcovered the effects of fancy and ſelf-deceit, ſince they were ſatisfied to have avoided ſenſual extravagancies, abandoning themſelves on the other ſide, under pretence of zeal for religion, to pride, envy, and a ſpirit of perſecution. This abuſe repreſented to me religion as an impoſture, which had always been more hurtful to human ſociety, than all irregular enjoyment of ſenſual pleaſures. Imagination overlooks the means, and when it employs its powers with too much vivacity on the object, frequently . through want of attention .chuſes the wrong ones. To apply the truth of religion carefully to oneſelf, to be honeſt and comply with the duties of our ſituation in life, I think moſt neceſſary to entitle a man to the name of a chriſtian. In this view I have wrote this with pleaſure. I ſubmit it, my dear friend, to your judgment, and leave it to you to make that uſe of it which you think beſt.

April the 23d, 1772.

STRUENSEE.

THE

HISTORY

OF

Count Enevold Brandt,

During the Time of his IMPRISONMENT
until his DEATH.

WRITTEN BY

The Reverend D. HEE.

ADVERTISEMENT.

The public may rely on the authenticity of the following account. It is beyond a doubt that D. Hee drew it up, and published it himself, for reasons which he mentions in the course of his narration. If the doctor should not answer the expectations we might have of him as a writer, the translator hopes, that his character as an honest man, and as a well-meaning divine, together with the subject of the narrative, will make some amends for it.

Count Enevold de Brandt.

Engraved for the History of Count Brandt.

HISTORY

O F

Count Enevold Brandt, &c.

THE sentiments and the conduct of the unhappy Count Brandt, during the time of
his imprifonment, were quite different from what
they were in his profperity, in which he offended
all well inclined people. His behaviour was
very edifying to thofe that had an opportunity of
converfing with him, in the latter part of his
life, and who have fincerity enough to own,
that he was very much humbled, and that the
words of our Saviour to St. Peter were applicable to him, when he fays: ‘ When thou art

con-

converted, ftrengthen thy brethren.' He fhewed himfelf in this character to all the officers that had the watch over him.

Since he was made prifoner of ftate, and even now after his death, many unjuft, and, God knows, very untrue reports have been fpread, as if his repentance had been hypocrify, and his fortitude and chearfulnefs when he died, temerity and prefumption. I have always contradicted fuch reports, and I do it now. Since I am fully convinced of the contrary, my confcience will not permit me to keep filence, but rather to declare, that the alteration of his fentiments was unfeigned, and that he hearkened to the invitations of the Gofpel. I do this with fo much the more readinefs, fince I believe that the greateft part of what has been faid, has proceeded from a zeal to promote the caufe of infidelity. There is a fet of people, who think it their duty to defend incredulity, even at the expence of truth and confcience. They have affiduoufly propagated every thing which has been faid about that levity of behaviour in the Count, which I myfelf obferved in the beginning, but which he owned and fo much repented of afterwards. I fhall not apologize for what might have happened before I came,

nor

nor for that which was viſible even in the beginning of my viſiting him; I rather ſhall praiſe
the mercy of God, which has ſhown its power
ſo ſurprizingly afterwards, and confirmed what
the Apoſtle ſays : ‘ Where ſin abounded, grace
did much more abound.’

Count Brandt received the beſt of educations. He
ſaw none but good examples in the houſe of his
parents, who had choſen the beſt tutors to form
his young heart for the fear of God.   He himſelf was ſenſible of this in his priſon, and aſſured
me that he very often had felt the power of the
converting grace of God within his ſoul.   He
recollected in particular the time when he was
firſt admitted to the Lord’s Supper, by the Rev.
Mr. Piper, at Copenhagen; at which time, according to his own words, he received the ſa-
crament with a fervent devotion : he added, he
could never forget the words of the clergyman,
which made ſo great an impreſſion upon his
mind : ‘ Hold that faſt which thou haſt, that
no man take thy crown.’

On the 23d of February, the Right Reverend the Biſhop Harboe ſent me, the King’s
own orders, whereby I was deſired to viſit

Count

Count Brandt, who was prisoner in the castle *.
I was not over-pleased with this charge, knowing
too well the sentiments and the former life of
the Count. He had been the greatest volup-
tuary, and a friend to all those vices which are
generally annexed to this character, and one
that turned every part of religion into ridicule.

The next day I was introduced to him by General Hoben, as the clergyman with whom
he might speak about religion. He received
me with great civility, and I, on my side, af-
sured him how much I sympathized with him
in his misfortunes. I wanted to gain his confidence, and therefore asked him, how he could
support himself in his distressed condition? He
said, " His mind was very much composed
and calm;" to which I replied: that it was a
great advantage he enjoyed, and that I wished
his ease of mind might be built upon a good
foundation; upon which I took an opportunity
to speak of religion as the only source of com-

---

* General lieutenant Hoben, the commander of the
castle, had asked Count Brandt: If he desired to converse
with a divine? His answer was, he had no objection to it,
but he should like to know who was to be the clergyman,
that was to attend him. He was told that this entirely
depended on the will of the king.

fort.

fort. He then faid, " That, he believed, the report that he had no religion, had reached me likewife." I faid, I could not deny this; and I was therefore the more forry, fince he wanted what was moft neceffary, and what could be moft ufeful to him both at prefent and in futurity.

" He then affured me that he never had been entirely without religion, though he muft own that he did not fpeak always with due refpect of it."

Finding that he had no intention to conceal his former way of thinking, I therefore afked him, if he fhould not like that we might be left alone to carry on our converfation by ourfelves. He faid, " He was ready for it." I then defired the officer who was upon watch, and who was with him day and night, to leave the room; which was the cafe afterwards always whenever I came. I now reminded him of what he had told me before, that he never had been without a fenfe of religion, not even then when he ridiculed it.

He confirmed what he had faid, but owned that he had feveral doubts about religion. I

told

told him that doubting was very natural to us, and even good chriftians now and then might be made uneafy by doubts, but that it was finful to raife doubts, and entertain them with delight.

His doubts were about the fall of man, original fin, and fome other matters concerning religion. When I had given him an anfwer to thefe doubts, I exhorted him to leave his carelefs way of thinking, and not to obftruct the way to truth, by wilfully prejudicing himfelf againft it. He faid, " That he had formerly talked very freely againft religion, but that many things he had faid, were only produced by a defire of fhewing himfelf witty."

When I exhorted him, fince he faw himfelf how badly he had acted, and into what mifery he by his contempt of religion had thrown himfelf, to mind now the time which was left him, and to look out for the falvation of his foul, he feemed to be greatly moved: particularly when I put him in mind of that good education he had enjoyed in the houfe of his parents, who took all poffible care to prevent the ruin of his foul. When I reprefented to him the tears of his pious mother, on account of the unhappy

condition

condition he was in, and the dangerous situation of his foul, he burft out into tears, fo that I myfelf began to be very much moved. Many more things being faid, and exhortations given, I took my leave of him, afking if it would be agreeable to him, that I fhould call again? To which he replied : " He fhould be glad to fee me at any time."

I left him with good hopes, and heard foon after of the effects of my vifit; for his levity, to which he was even in his prifon addicted, feemed to be checked. According to the account given to the commander of the caftle by the officer who had the watch, he not only had been very quiet, but had alfo burft out in tears for very near an hour and a half together, fitting all the while on his bed.—But as foon as he had eafed his mind by his tears, his levity appeared again, for he fang an air afterwards. This, however, did not difcourage me, nor abate my hopes. I vifited him the next day again, and found that my vifits were really not difagreeable to him; for he faid, " He had longed to fee me."

Our converfation of this day turned upon feveral religious fubjects. I exhorted him to make the beft ufe of his time, and to turn his thoughts towards God; and for this very reafon I ftrongly

recom-

recommended prayer to him. I affured him that I had prayed fervently to God that he might fave his foul, and I fhould continue doing the fame. He thanked me for this, and acknowledged, that the compaffion for him which I had fhewn the day before, had gained me his heart, and had made me dear to him. I fpoke feveral things after this, and found that my exhortations had fome effect upon him, for he very feldom, when I was with him, even to the laft day of his life, was without tears in his eyes, fo often as I fpoke to him about his former life, the depravity of his heart, and the greatnefs of God's mercy.—He owned that he earneftly defired the pardon of God, through Chrift his Redeemer, of which he, as he himfelf faid, ftood greatly in need; although the natural difpofition of his heart might not be bad, yet it would not juftify him before God, in whofe eyes he muft appear as a very great finner.

In the mean time a rumour was fpread, and I heard of it, that he, even in my prefence, with another perfon who fat next him, had made ufe of words which betrayed the great levity of his mind. I was very forry to hear fuch things, and the next time I faw him, I very earneftly fpoke to him about this report, and appealed

5

pealed to his own confcience, whether he had been guilty of fuch a thing or not. He feemed to be affected on the occafion, and declared " He was not forry on account of what the people faid; it grieved him rather that I myfelf fhould entertain fuch thoughts of him." I affured him it was no pleafure to me to entertain them, but my confcience obliged me to admonifh him concerning this report, that I might fpare myfelf any future uneafinefs about it. However, he owned, " That it was poffible *fuch words* might have efcaped him, on account of the levity of his heart, but he hinted, that fome perfon or other, that wanted to bring fuch reports among the people, had given him an occafion for it, of which he made ufe, whilft his heart was not upon its guard."—I exhorted him to beg God to forgive him this tranfgreffion, and to be watchful over himfelf, that if opportunities fhould offer themfelves of committing fuch an action again, he might refift in time: that he had better give no anfwer at all to things which might induce him to exert his vanity, but rather fhew himfelf a penitent finner, who was as anxious to edify others by his converfation now, as he formerly had been to corrupt them by it.—He anfwered, " He was not able yet to fhew himfelf as a religious man before others, but he fhould follow

my

my advice, and give no anfwer to things that could difhonour himfelf and others."—I could defire of him no more at prefent, but exhorted him to fearch diligently the wretchednefs of his moral condition, and to pray to God to affift him in this felf examination.

I could eafily imagine, that in my abfence, when he had nothing to entertain himfelf with, his former vanity and levity would return again; I therefore offered to bring him fome religious books, that he might improve in what is good. He thanked me for it, and defired I would not forget it.

When I paid him my next vifit, I brought him the tranflation of *Gibfon*'s Paftoral Letters, for I thought this book might be ufeful to him on account of the folid arguments it contains for the truth of the chriftian religion, particularly fince the Count had formerly pretended to be a freethinker and a deift; I gave him likewife fome of Dr. *Doddridge*'s writings. He took thefe books with a kind of eagernefs, and told me afterwards that he had been edified by them. I likewife brought him a Bible, and heard at another time that, according to his own confeffion, the 53d chapter of the prophet Ifaiah, and the 13th of St. Luke had made a great impreffion

preffion upon him. He read fome Pfalms of David to me, and defired me to explain feveral paffages which he did not quite underftand. I did it, and he feemed to be pleafed, for during the whole time I was fitting by his fide, he would fix his eyes very attentively upon me. Now and then he would ftart fome objections, but I cannot fay that they ever fhewed any levity of heart, or the leaft of malice, but rather tended to a defire of better information.—He begged of me to bring him *Hervey's Meditations*, and *Newton on Prophecies*, as the latter is tranflated into Danifh by Commodore Effura. He told me afterwards that the reading of thefe books had much edified him, particularly the latter, fince it contained fuch clear proofs of the divinity of the Scriptures, upon which all religion is built.

However, the reports of his pretended levity did not ceafe, and that his conduct in my abfence was quite different from that when I was prefent: yet I found thefe reports, from the following reafons, to be falfe, and that they were the idle invention of ill-meaning people. The converfations we had together convince me that his expreffions were the fentiments of his heart, which began to be averfe to worldly things. Befides, I enquired of the honeft and venerable commander of the caftle,

caftle, if any one of the officers that guarded him, and who were to give an account of him every morning, had mentioned any thing to this purpofe ? He affured me it was all falfe, and that the Count, fince I had brought him thefe books, had amufed himfelf with them, and that he fcarcely ever laid the Bible out of his hands; for which reafon he very feldom fpoke of any thing elfe, much lefs of any thing that could give offence. The alteration of his fentiments appeared likewife, as the commander obferved, from his behaviour before the committee that fat on his affairs, who teftified that he not only freely anfwered the queftions laid before him, but that he even confeffed more than he was requefted to do. The commander added, that if any thing indecent had happened, he would have informed me of it. I was pleafed to hear this, and I was ftill more fo, fince every one of the officers that had been upon watch affured me, that his converfation was not only decent, but likewife oftentimes edifying; for he frequently reprefented to them what comforts religion adminiftered to a man who was convinced of its truth and importance; it was the only means to make our minds compofed, which happinefs he enjoyed, and was indebted for it to religion. He affured them, that during his
profperity,

profperity, and in the enjoyment of all luftful pleafures, he felt no real fatisfaction of mind.

I was ftill more convinced of the falfity of thefe reports, fince fome things were faid to have happened whilft I was with him, which I knew were not true. It was faid, for inftance, that when I was once with him, I, according to cuftom, had found him very devout; but when I had left the prifon, I had liftened at the door, which was bolted, and hearing from within fome things which betrayed his levity, I had returned to him again, and reproached. him on account of his conduct. This report, which, in fome refpects, concerned myfelf, convinced me clearly by its untruth, that fome malicious perfons invented and propagated all thefe ftories, for the fake of rendering the reverence the Count paid to religion fufpicious, left his example might open the eyes of thofe profeffing his former principles. The Count himfelf hinted to me, that a certain perfon, whom he named, had propagated the moft wicked and low expreffions, which he was faid to have dropped on account of his approaching death and execution. This fame man, or fomebody elfe like him, has given out, that I had denied giving the facrament to the Count, becaufe his heart was fo hardened. How great

an

an untruth this is, the remainder of my narrative will shew.

I now was fully satisfied on account of these reports, and exhorted him to go on in the manner he had begun, till he had finished his course. I heard with pleasure, that he became a preacher of repentance himself. With great freedom he owned now before me and others, that his imprisonment was the means of setting his soul at liberty, and he found his chains so little troublesome to him, that he would often-times take them up and kiss them. " For, said he, when I believed myself to be free, I was a miserable slave to my passions; and now, since I am a prisoner, truth and grace have set me at liberty." He further pitied the miserable condition of those that were under the yoke of unbelief and sin, which he himself had worn, and kept himself in it by reading deistical writings. He mentioned, among the rest, the works of Voltaire, to whom he owed very little that was good. He said, he had spent upon his travels four days with this old advocate for unbelief, and had heard nothing from him but what could corrupt the heart and found morals. He was very sorry for all this, but was much pleased that he had found a taste for the true word of God, whose

I   efficacy

efficacy upon his heart, since he read it with good intentions, convinced him of its divine origin. On this occasion he spoke of Struensee, and said, he was a man without any religion, who, from his infancy, according to his own confession, never had any impression or feelings of it. As to himself, he assured me, that though he had been far from being virtuous, yet he always entertained a secret reverence for religion, and had spoken several times about it to Struensee, in hopes of bringing him to better sentiments, but he never would hear him. It appeared to me a little odd, that the blind should thus have led the blind : I therefore answered nothing, thinking it might perhaps be his self-conceit that made him speak so, or that he wanted to make me entertain a better opinion of his errors than I had reason for, therefore I would not tempt him to support an untruth by defending what he had told me. But I found afterwards that he had spoken the truth, when I was desired by D. Munter, in the name of Struensee, to come to him, as he had something to tell me, which was to be communicated to Count Brandt. The commander of the castle told me this message of D. Munter, and my answer was, that I was ready to call upon Struensee, if he (the commander) and D. Munter would be present. My request was granted, and

and I came to Struensee, who received me very civilly, and gave me a long account of his former bad principles, (which, in short, were nothing else but mere *materialismus* and *mechanismus*, according to the system of *de la Mettrie* *) and told me, lastly, what I was to tell Count Brandt. The contents of the message were, that he was convinced, by the grace of God, and by reading the Bible, of the divine authority of the Scriptures; and that I might tell Count Brandt of this alteration of his, which, he hoped, would be agreeable to him. He added, which I shall mention in his own words,

" I confess that Brandt has spoken frequently to me about religion, but I always desired him to keep silence on this head." By this I found, that what Brandt had told me concerning Struensee was true †. I brought the message I was charged with by Struensee directly to Brandt. He rejoiced inwardly on account of this news,

---

* *De la Mettrie* died at Berlin in 1751. His famous book, *L'homme Machine*, makes man a mere machine, and his soul an insignificant word. The powers of the soul he thinks to be nothing else but an unknown motion of the brain. His *Traité de la vie heureuse*, contains the consequences of this system. He denies the immortality of the soul, laughs at all religion, and places all human happiness in the enjoyment of sensual pleasures.

† See the foregoing History of the Conversion of Count Struensee, p. 79, 83.

desired

defired me to go to Struenfee again, and tell him that it gave him great pleafure to hear that he had embraced truth, and that he begged of him to adhere to it to the laft. He added: " Tell Struenfee, on my part, that my own experience has now taught me, that true eafe of mind is no where to be found, but in Chrift crucified."—I carried this meffage back again to Struenfee, who feemed to be much pleafed at it.

As I kept no journal of the fubjects of our many conferences, I fhall not attempt a circumftantial detail of them. I had never an intention of publifhing this, if the aforementioned reports had not forced me to it.

The Count would frequently mention how unhappy his former condition had been; how great reafon he had to praife God's mercy that had faved his life at feveral times in moft imminent dangers, that he might not perifh for ever. He mentioned in particular one inftance, when he, laft fummer, was thrown from his horfe, taken up for dead, and laid four and twenty hours fpeechlefs. " Confider, faid he, where my poor foul would have gone to, if death had fnatched me away in the condition I was then in, for I was dead in fins; but God fpared me that I might come into this condition, and that my foul may be faved.

T

I exhorted him to pray frequently: He said, he did it very often, and looked upon it as a great mercy of God that he now confidered it as his duty to pray: but, he faid, he muft complain that his heart was often very cold, though he repented of his former way of life, and hoped for mercy upon no other foundation than Chrift's redemption. When I had comforted him in a manner I thought proper, he then told me, that he, one evening, after a fervent prayer, had found a great eafe of mind and comfort.

Towards the end of his life he declared, that during the time I had attended him, he had three different impediments to conquer, which he, at laft, through the affiftance of Chrift, overcame. The firft was, that it was hard for him to confefs that he really was fo great a finner as he afterwards did. The fecond was, to follow my advice, and to own before thofe that were about him the alteration of his fentiments. The third was of fuch a nature, that I dare not mention it, though it concerned his foul.—I found that thefe victories which he had gained over himfelf were not imaginary, but real ones : for he now was ready to open his heart, and to pour out what hitherto had lain concealed in it. He

spoke

fpoke without fear of his approaching death, and praifed the inward affurance he enjoyed of being pardoned before God, and of which mercy he acknowledged himfelf to be unworthy. " What have I deferved before God, faid he, but his eternal wrath ?"

The time when his fentence was to be given now drew near, but he appeared to be quite calm, for he was confident of the honefty of his judges, and that they would act no otherwife than according to law and confcience. I fhewed him that he was very right in this refpect, and that it was a proof of a Providence, that his judges were all fuch men, whofe knowledge of the law, and integrity of confcience, would not permit them to deviate the leaft from juftice, and that he might be affured, his fentence would be entirely agreeable to the tenor of the law. As much as he feemed to be refigned to his fate, yet it appeared to me as if he ftill entertained fome hopes of faving his life. Perhaps this was owing to the common rumour, that Count Brandt would come off without lofing his life, which fomebody had told him, and thereby revived the thought of efcaping the fcaffold. About four or five weeks before this, he was fo full of the hopes of a pardon, that he felt a paroxyfm of his former levity and ambition,

which

which made him defire of the royal commiffion to have his fetters taken off in a folemn manner, and to propofe to them fome other ftrange requefts. He himfelf, when I once took my leave of him, told me about it, and I did not chufe to give him a direct anfwer, becaufe I looked upon it as an attack of his former levity and precipitation. However, when I came again, I reminded him of what he had told me, and afked him, how he could entertain any fuch thought, which betrayed fo much of his attachment to the world ? I defired him to give this up entirely, fince he, in his prefent fituation, fhould endeavour to difengage himfelf from all worldly things. He took this advice not at all amifs, but owned, that the thought he had entertained was produced by his levity, to which fault he was fo much addicted, that he believed there were not ten people in the world equally fo with himfelf. I looked upon this confeffion, and the manner in which he took what I had faid, as a proof of the fincerity of his heart and his repentance. I told him likewife, on this occafion, how little foundation he had for entertaining any hopes of faving his life ; that his crimes were then indeed not publicly known, but that there was a public rumor in what they confifted ; and in cafe, faid I, you fhould fave your life, the greateft mercy that could be fhewn to

you,

you, would be the changing of your dead war-rant into imprifonment for life; and I defired him to confider which he fhould prefer. He anfwered, " That if God fhould forefee that, in cafe his life was faved, he fhould be carried away again by vanity and fin, he would pray of him not to fpare his life, but rather let him die; for it would be infinitely better for him to enter into a happy eternity and to be with Chrift, than to become again a flave of fin, and to lofe in this manner everlafting happinefs." He repeated this declaration, at the very time when he expected his fentence, in fuch expreffions which proved that the victory of grace and of faith was now become greater than before; for he faid, his prayers were now always after the manner in which Chrift prayed; " Not my will, but thine be done." " In cafe, faid he, it cannot be otherwife, and I cannot efcape death, I leave this world fully perfuaded that this is the will of God, who fees that I might be carried away again by the world, and, therefore, in mercy to me will prevent this."

I went to him on the 24th of April, the day when he was to receive his fentence. I found him lying upon his bed, and more thoughtful than common; but he got up directly, and I began to fpeak to him in a comforting manner,

T 3

that

that he had no reason to be fearful of his sentence in this world, since he knew his judgment in that which is to come, namely, a full pardon before God through Christ his Redeemer. He then, after some further conversation, promised that he would make himself easy and wait composedly for the will of God.

I heard the next day that sentence was not only given, but that it was also believed that the King would entirely confirm it. I therefore went to him, and found him, though he was fully informed of the manner of his death, as composed and calm as I had left him. I spoke several things that could afford him comfort, and he heard all that I said with pleasure, and asked me afterwards whether I had read his sentence? I told him, I had not, and knew no more of it than what the common report was. He then took a copy of the sentence out of the drawer of a table which stood next to him. When I had read it, I said many things to comfort him; and he seemed quite composed; and as he now had given over all hopes of saving his life, he resigned himself entirely to his fate, and seemed to be so full of his future happiness that I could not help admiring his peace of mind, which God had granted to him whose

sins

fins had been fo great. He himſelf was fenfible of this, for he derived from this grace of God, not only his tranquillity of mind but even his health. For when he enjoyed his liberty, he frequently was not well, but during the long time of his impriſonment, though he could fcarcely ftir or move, he had a good appetite, and flept well. He aſked me then what day his execution would take place, for he had heard that it was fixed for Thurfday the 30th of April. I told him that I was in this refpect as uninformed as he himfelf was; and the time of his departure muft be equally the fame to him, if he only knew he was ready.

The following day, which was Sunday, April the 26th, I received, juft when I came from church, a letter from Biſhop Harboe, wherein I was acquainted with the King's pleaſure, that both the ftate-prifoners fhould be executed on Tuefday next, April the 28th, and that I was accordingly to regulate my affairs in regard to Count Brandt. This news put my mind into a great emotion: I haftened foon to the poor Count. When I came to the caftle, I enquired of the commander, whether Brandt knew that his end was

fo

so near. He answered, he did not, and he himself knew nothing of it, but thought he should receive orders for it that very evening; which was the case. I therefore myself was to acquaint him with this melancholy news, and I did it in the following manner. Since I came to him to day rather earlier than usual, I told him I should make the best of his time since it was so short. He guessed from what I said that I knew the time of his execution, and asked when it was to be? I told him it was the day after to-morrow, when he should be delivered from all evil. He heard it unconcerned, and said he readily submitted to the will of God. I then prepared him for receiving the sacrament, after which I took my leave.

I came on Monday about ten o'clock in the forenoon, and when I had spoke to him about the sacrament, I made a proposal to him, which I left to himself either to accept or not. I said, he knew how many bad reports were spread of his behaviour during the time of his imprisonment; I therefore left it to him to consider whether it might not be of use to make a declaration before proper witnesses, what his real sentiments were. He readily complied with the proposal, and I went to the commander of
the

the caftle, who came with four gentlemen officers more, in whofe prefence he declared, that
he was ready to die and was not afraid of it; he
likewife confeffed before the All-knowing God,
that he without hypocrify had fought for God's
mercy; he likewife confeffed, as he had done
before, that he had acted very inconfiderately,
that his levity had been very great, and that he,
on this account, acknowledged God's mercy,
in fuffering him to die, left he fhould be drawn
away again from religion. He faid, he knew
very well, that the fame levity of temper had
induced him, in the beginning of his imprifonment, to talk in a manner he was now afhamed
of; though he was fure in his confcience that
many untruths were invented and propagated
among the people; but he forgave thofe who
had been guilty of fuch a thing. Now he wifhed
that thofe gentlemen that were prefent would
bear teftimony to what he fhould fay. He
then acknowledged himfelf a great finner before God, a finner who had gone aftray, but
was brought back by Chrift. He then begged
the commander and the other officers to forgive
him, if by his levity he had offended any one of
them, and wifhed that God's mercy in Chrift
might always attend them as the greateft bleffing. He fpoke all this with fuch a readinefs

and

and in so moving terms, that all who were present were affected by it, and every one of them wished that God would preserve him in this situation of mind to the last. When the gentlemen were gone, I administered the sacrament to him, and he appeared as penitent and as devout as I have at any time seen any christian whatever. When I approached to give him the sacrament, he turned in the chair as if he would face me, and I, thinking he meant only to make it more commodious to me to give it him, desired him to sit still; but he said, " He would try to kneel down," which he did, and received the sacrament with so many tears and with such signs of inward hope, that I could not help being greatly affected.

I left him about noon, but came again in the afternoon, when I found him quite composed without any fear of death. I spent all the time I was with him in devotion, and left him late in the evening.

On Tuesday the 28th of April, which was the day of his execution, and as I firmly believed of his entrance into the bliss of eternity, I came to him early in the morning, about six o'clock.

o'clock. I afked him directly how he did, and how he had refted that night. He faid, " He was very well, and had refted well." I anfwered, I was glad to hear it, for if the body had had its reft, his foul would be the more ferene to enter upon its journey. He prayed a long while in my prefence very fervently. He fhewed him-felf in his expreffions a humble and penitent finner, but at the fame time one who entertains the fureft hopes of being pardoned before God. He prayed for the church of Chrift, for the King and the nation, for all that were mifled by error and irreligion. Laftly, he prayed to God to forgive him all that whereby he had offended others, and expreffed how readily he for-gave thofe that were his enemies. He thanked God for all the mercies he had fhewn him during the time of his imprifonment; he prayed for me likewife. Then he read the Lord's prayer with much attention, adding now and then an ex-planation to what he had been reading, infomuch that I was amazed to fee how great his prefence of mind was when he was juft going to die. When he was pronouncing the words, ' Thy kingdom come,' he added: " Yes, now it is coming." When he read, ' Forgive us our trefpaffes, as we forgive them that trefpafs

againft

againſt us,' He added: " Thou O God and my Redeemer, who knoweſt my own heart and that of all men, thou knoweſt how free my heart is from all hatred and malice againſt any perſon whatever, and that I wiſh well to every body in this and the future world."

When he had finiſhed his prayers, his chains, which were fixed in the wall, were taken off, and he put thoſe clothes on in which he intended to appear on the ſcaffold. He then drank a diſh of coffee and eat ſomething, walking up and down in the room, which he could not do before. As often as I aſked him how he found himſelf, he ſaid, he was not afraid of dying. He afterwards aſked me, whether I had ſeen any body executed before, and how far he was to lay his body bare for execution?

Soon after, the door of the priſon was opened, and an officer deſired me to get into a coach that was to carry me before him to the place of execution. I then recommended him to the mercy of God, who was ready and powerful to ſtrengthen to the laſt. He then embraced me, and we parted, till we met again at the place of execution.

When

When I received him there, I comforted him, and faid, among other words, that Chrift would not leave him. Upon which he anfwered: " He has been with me all the way hither." We then went up the ftairs to the fcaffold. Even here, he affured me his mind was compofed, and he was not afraid of death. I fpoke feveral things after his fentence was read to him, and his coat of arms broken. And when I happened to quote the words, ' Son, be of good cheer, thy fins are forgiven thee,' he faid : " Yes, they all are caft into the depths of the fea."

When I had read thofe things from the ritual which are ufual on fuch occafions, and had afked him, if he acknowledged the juftice of his, fentence? and when he had anfwered, " Yes," he then began to pray that God would blefs the King and the whole land for Chrift's fake. Several prayers being offered up on my part, I gave him the benediction, and taking him by the hand, delivered him up to juftice. He quickly pulled his clothes off, laid himfelf down, and when his head was already upon the block, and I reminded him of Jefus falling on his face in Gethfemane praying, he

3   faid :

said: " The blood of Chrift interceedeth for me." Whilft I was faying: ' O Chrift, in thee I live, in thee I die; O thou Lamb of God that takeft away the fins of the world, be merciful,' he fuffered his punifhment.

Two anonymous LETTERS *to Count* BRANDT, *which were found in the pocket-book which he ufed always to carry about him, wherein he was forewarned of what happened to him many months after.*

* * * * *

Sir,

' " Perhaps you may wonder to receive a letter without a name on a matter of fo great importance, from a friend who formerly ufed to tell you the truth before your face; but the times we live in now, will not juftify a man in expofing himfelf to danger, without feeing any good arifing from it.

The two laft court-days, I fought for an opportunity at Hirfchholm to fpeak a few words to you in private; but I found it was impoffible. You might have obferved this, if you had been at all attentive; but I found you fo much engaged with another object, that I could not

approach

I

approach you near enough to make you underftand what I wanted : and I thought it not ad-
vifable to go to Hirfchholm on purpofe to pay
you a vifit.

Once, Sir, you fhewed that you had the honour of your mafter at heart. It was then
afferted, that neither zeal nor attachment were
the fprings of your actions, but ambition and
intereft, becaufe you hoped that if you could
bring into difgrace Count H—— you might
fucceed him in that favour and honour he enjoyed. However, the bulk of the people
thought your intentions noble and without felf-
intereft. Perhaps the immediate confequences
of this your tranfaction have made fo great an
impreffion upon you, that you think you dare
not venture upon fuch another. And yet the
final iffue of the affair has fhewn, that even your
ill fuccefs in it has been more advantageous to
you than detrimental. Therefore, Sir, do not
think that this was the mere effect of accident,
but rather that a higher hand has guided this
matter. I do not know what your notions of
God may be, or whether you believe a God at
all, or only a mere Stoic fate. It would be very
fuperfluous to debate a matter of fo great importance here. Time will come, when experience

will teach you that there is a God, who sees and knows every thing, who either early or late rewards virtue and punishes vice.

My intention is not at present to make you a christian. It is only to remind you of your duty, that duty, which even an honest heathen thought himself obliged to, towards his King, his country, himself and his family. The heathen laws demanded this of every subject and of every man who laid any claim to honour.

You see, Sir, in what manner your King and benefactor is used. You see the indecent things that are done before his eyes, and in which you yourself are too much concerned. You see that in the whole kingdom every thing is turned upside down. Consider, Sir, and recover your senses, and you will not be at a loss how to act. If it is true, (and it is but too true) that the life of the King is in danger, or at least, that preparations are making to take away his liberty; you certainly must know it. The sense of the nation on this head cannot be unknown to you, and that one time or other you are to account for the life and liberty of your Sovereign. You, Sir, since you are constantly about him,

and

and since you see and know of every thing; be assured that your head will be answerable for it either sooner or later. Think of your own safety, I conjure you by the friendship I entertain for you. It is in your power to do it. You see plainly from the desire of the King to avoid the place and company in which he is ill-used, and from his aversion to return to it, that he is sensible of the ill-treatment. He one time or another will deliver himself from you, or good fortune will rid him of you, and what will then be your fate? Would it not be best for you, to save your head, and to do at the same time your duty? To build your happiness on a solid and noble foundation, which you then will owe to your zeal, your faithfulness and attachment to your King, who will reward you with riches and honour, and the nation will not think even this an equivalent for your services. You and your present welfare depends on the caprice of a wretch who will abandon you as soon as he is above your assistance. At present he makes use of you as the monkey did of the cat, and I fancy you have found this out more than once if you will not impose upon yourself.

If the King should come to town, I advise you to act in this manner. Prevail upon him

to

to go to the palace, and perfuade him to call
for one or two of his faithful fervants to con-
fult in what manner to proceed. It is unfortunate enough that the number of thefe faithful
fervants is fo fmall, and reduced perhaps to one
or two perfons ; for the beft and cievereft men
are carefully removed. You will eafily guefs
who thefe perfons are without my naming them.
Perfeverance, honefty, and experience are cha-
racteriftics by which you are to know them. I
could name them, but I would avoid the leaft
fufpicion of felf-intereft. However, I muft tell
you, that it is neither ——— nor ———; both
are detefted by the nation to an equal degree.
You will forfeit your head if you do not follow
this advice, which I give you as your friend,
and a faithful fervant of the King. If you do
not mind it, but neglect your duty towards
your King and benefactor, you may be fure
it will coft you your life, your honour, and
every thing which is deareft to an honeft man,
and befides no body will pity you. If you, on
the other fide, do what your duty requires, and
fave your King from thofe wicked hands he is
fallen into, you may be fure that there is no
honour or profperity to which you would not be
entitled to, and this with confent of the King
and all his faithful fubjects.

Perhaps

Perhaps you will think proper to fhew this letter to your Struenfee, to give him a proof of your faithfulnefs, at the expence of thofe obligations you have fworn to your King, and to induce him to grant new favours to the hufband of Lady ———; and perhaps he might do it, to deceive you, and to keep you in his intereft. But I affure you that if they have got rid of the King, you will be wretched, and perhaps the guilt will fall upon you.

I repeat it again, your head fhall anfwer for the fafety of the King. You are continually about him, you accompany him, you are intrufted with his perfon. And left you may plead ignorance, I affure you upon honour, that in fuch cafe, the copy of this letter fhall be produced againft you in proper time and place. And for fear you fhould miftake in this refpect, I defire you to mind the feal of this letter, which contains the initial letters of my name, and which will alfo be produced againft you.

The life and health of the King, together with the welfare of the kingdom, are in your hands; act in a manner that you can anfwer for before your fellow-citizens, I will not fay before God, (for I do not know what your idea

of

of God may be, though I have reafon to think, from what you told me once in your apartments at Chriftianfburg, and afterwards at Hirfchholm, that your notions are not altogether as they fhould be.)

You fee I am not afraid of your gueffing who I am, and I affure you, that if you act as I expect from your birth, you will find me to be your faithful and devoted fervant."

July the 8th, 1771.

━━━━━━━━━━

" Well, Sir, what I foretold you has happened, and you feel already the effects of your bad conduct. You have been faithlefs to your King, and you are now treated by others in the fame manner. They ufe you as the monkey did the cat. You are deceived, and fince they find they can do with you whatever they pleafe, they laugh at you now, and it will not laft long before they will fend you with contempt about your bufinefs; and left you fhould tell tales, they very likely may imprifon you for life, or fend you, by fome means or other, into another world. This will be the due reward of your treachery, cowardice, and your mean actions. I prognofticated all thefe things to you in my laft letter of July the 8th: fince that time, my friendfhip for you, of which
I have

I have given you undeniable proofs, is grown very cool; you do not deserve that it should continue, since you have been unable to follow good advice, and to do what your honour and your duty requires of you; you rather have chosen to persevere in your wicked way of life. If you, at that time, had followed my advice, you would have set the King at liberty by saving him, and your praise would have been immortal: you then would have satisfied the duties of a good subject, of a faithful servant, and of an honest man: you would have gained the applause, not only of all your countrymen, but even of all Europe: they would all have united to procure you rewards according to your merit, and proportionable to the services done to the King and your country. And certainly nobody would have been more deserving of rewards. But now you are detested through the whole kingdom, and every where you are laughed at. Much was expected from your loyalty, your love for the King, and from a sense of your own duty; but people were mistaken. You are now punished; you are infamous among the whole nation, and your name is mentioned with horror. At court you are laughed at, and entertained with vain hopes; an imaginary greatness is shewn you, you are tickled with the empty title of Count, which will remain a monument of

U 3

your

your want of faith, your weaknefs, your meannefs, and your reproachful conduct. In the
mean time Struenfee infults the King and the
whole royal family, not becaufe they had offended him, but only to fhew his unlimited
power. He arrogates all honours to himfelf;
he makes himfelf mafter of the government,
the concerns of the kingdom, and of the
King himfelf, whom he difhonours before the
whole world; he difpofes of the revenues of the
kingdom in a defpotic manner, and againft all
order. This wretch durft attempt to put himfelf
on a level with his mafter, by drawing up an
order, by which the figning of his name obtains
the fame authority, which, according to the
conftitution of the kingdom, only belongs to the
fignature of the King. Your meannefs, and
your unwarrantable conduct, have affifted to raife
him fo high; you could have prevented this,
and therefore you will be anfwerable for the confequences. He commits crimes, and affaffinations,
and he does it to keep the reins of government;
but you contribute your fhare, by obeying the
orders of this Cromwell, who is ready to facrifice the life of the King a thoufand times over,
if poffible, that he may obtain his wicked ends,
and provide for his own fecurity. Inftead of ac-
quainting the King with things which nobody
knows better than you, (for you are cunning
enough

enough when it concerns your own intereſt) you aſſiſt this *Dick leat the buſh* in arrogating to himſelf royal authority ; in keeping his maſter under guardianſhip ; in degrading him in the eyes of his ſubjects, that their love may ceaſe, or at leaſt decreaſe ; and laſtly, as every one ſays, in uſing him perſonally ill in the bargain.

You that can prevent all this, and ſave the King from the hands of this good-for-nothing wretch, and yet are not willing to do it, you, Sir, are accountable for it, and you deſerve greater puniſhment than the traitor himſelf : and believe me, as ſure as that there is a God, you ſooner or later, ſhall pay for it with your head.

You ſee how prepoſterouſly buſineſs is tranſacted ; every thing is overthrown and jumbled together in the moſt ſtrange manner, and blended with the higheſt inconſiderateneſs, of which there is no parallel inſtance to be met with in hiſtory. The moſt honeſt people that have ſerved the kingdom ſuch a long while and ſo faithfully that even envy itſelf could not blame them, are removed at a diſtance : they are turned way in the moſt ſhameful manner, if they will not fall in with the meaſures of this *Doctor of phyſic*, or if he is afraid of their honeſty. Their places are filled up with wretches who know nothing of the conſtitution of the kingdom and of the ſituation of affairs ;

who

who know nothing of the bufinefs annexed to their offices; in fhort, people of whom nobody fo much as dreamt that they were acquainted even with the firft principles of the art of government.

For God's fake! what is the meaning that a ————— and ————, profeffor of mathematics at Ligniz, is placed at the head of the board of finances? Thefe men enjoy a yearly falary of 3000 rixdollars, whilft others that have ferved forty or fifty years without blame, are now ftarving, becaufe they could not betray the King and their country, and would not be employed in promoting bad and deftructive ends. Yet thefe ignorant men dare to take upon their fhoulders a burden under which, particularly in thefe unhappy times, a man of courage, abilities, and experience would have trembled. However, the wife man knows the danger, and therefore will not hazard the welfare of the nation and his good character; but the ignorant man who has nothing to lofe, does not perceive the unhappy confequences of his inability and ignorance.

You fee, Sir, that the nation is acquainted with the wretchednefs of this prefent adminiftration, that it feels the bad confequences of it, which will drive it at laft to extremities. You may be affured of the truth of this the more, fince difcontent

content difcovers itfelf in a public and an alarming manner. You know all this, but you conceal it from the King, though you are the only man that converfes with the King, whilft accefs to the throne is denied to all the reft of his fubjects. You alone can inform the King of the dangerous fituation he himfelf and his kingdoms are in. The inconceivable indifference wherewith the beft and braveft of the King's fubjects are treated, fhews that a certain kingdom (Norway) may foon become alienated; fo that, in a fhort time, every thing may be loft without help, if his Majefty continues to hearken to fuch b..d advice.

You fee, Sir, how the department of foreign affairs is managed, and how, by the intrigues and incapacity of our *great prime minifter*, who has the audacity to interfere, every thing is perplexed, fo that the name of the Danes is now a fubject for ridicule.

You fee, Sir, and you know, how arbitrarily his *excellency cur great prime minifter, Count Struenfee,* difpofes of the finances—the pure blood of the poor fubjects.

You, Sir, as you are a Dane, of noble extraction, beloved by your King, to whom you
and

and your family owe fo many favours; and yet for you to keep filence!—Do not you blufh? and are you not convinced in your confcience, that you yourfelf ought to fall the firft facrifice of fuch conduct, fince you might have prevented all this, or had, at leaft, a thoufand opportunities to fet things to rights again?

If tumult and rebellion (which God forbid) fhould be the confequences, of whom do you think the exafperated populace would take hold firft? Would not they fecure you firft, fince you are, at leaft, as culpable as Struenfee? And do not you expofe your life, fooner or later, to the greateft danger by this conduct, which is not confiftent with the character of an honeft man?

Reflect, Sir, and return to your duty: I conjure you by the afhes of your father, whom you never knew; by the tears of your virtuous mother, who weeps, perhaps, already on account of your approaching untimely death; and what is ftill more, I conjure you by the tears, which, perhaps, one time may be fhed, on your account, by the King, the royal family, and your afflicted country.

You are not afraid to difagree with the *Doctor-prime-minifter* when it concerns your private intereft;

reft; but you are mean enough to be reconciled by a prefent of 10,000 rixdollars, of which he has robbed the King and the nation to give them to you. Are you not afhamed of fuch a meannefs? and are you afraid of this man in matters that concern the welfare of your King and your country? Thefe traitors and villains, who defend a bad caufe, would not have courage to oppofe you, through fear of endangering their heads, which already fit loofely upon their fhoulders. You would fave your King and your country; you would deferve rewards, and would have a right to claim them; they would follow you of courfe, fince nobody would refufe them: I myfelf, who write this letter, would be the firft that would contribute largely towards loading you with riches. With what tranquillity and inward fatisfaction would you enjoy your fortune, your prerogatives, and your honour, if you fhould gain this by the confent, and even agreeably to the wifhes of your King, your country, and your fellow citizens. I defire you, Sir, to confider this well, though I entertain a better opinion of your generofity, than to fuppofe that you are to be inftigated to perform noble actions only by mercenary motives.

In my opinion you muft begin this important bufinefs in the following manner. You are frequently alone with the King: you take a walk in

the

the evening with the King, as I was informed laſt
Wedneſday at Hirſchholm : you have found that
the King is weary of the guardianſhip he is kept
under.   Make uſe, Sir, of ſuch a favorable moment, or occaſion it yourſelf, ſince you have
underſtanding enough for it.   Repreſent to
him the unhappy ſituation he is in, and how
inconſiſtent it is with thoſe obligations his royal
dignity lays him under.   Tell him that he, by
ſigning the order of the 15th of July, has divided
the throne and his royal authority between himſelf and Struenſee; that he himſelf, the royal family, the kingdom, all his ſubjects, his revenues, the life and the property of every one,
are left to the arbitrary diſpoſal of this *arch-grand-
vizir,* who is a man without experience, without
honour, without religion, without fidelity; who
does not regard laws, who is maſter over all, even
over the life of the King.   You know that great
crimes are oftentimes productive of ſtill greater
ones, or that we at leaſt muſt fear that it might
happen.   When you have explained this to the
King, then repreſent to him the deſpair his ſubjects are in, and to what they might be driven by
ſuch a deſtructive adminiſtration, and by ſuch
miſery.   Shew him what danger threatens him
and his empire, if this wretch has time enough
to turn every thing upſide down.   If you ſhould
put the heart of the King in emotion, and ſhould

have

have convinced him, how abfolutely neceffary it was, to think of the prefervation of his royal per- fon, his family, and his kingdom; then pro- pofe to him to go directly to Copenhagen, where he will be quite fafe; to refort to the palace, and to fend for two or three noblemen that can give good advice, according as the circumftances re- quire; that he might not take falfe fteps (which could be of confequence) at the time when the nation fhould attempt to revenge itfelf, and to fhew its hatred againft the authors of its misfor- tunes and its miferies. I could name thefe perfons, but the nation will do it for me; they ought to be perfons acquainted with government, that they may advife according as the prefent fituation of affairs requires: but it muft not be ———, nor ———, nor ———, for thefe three the nation equally detefts, and they, there- fore, would fruftrate the whole defign.

For God's, your King's, your country's, your family's, your own fake, confider all this well, and do not delay any longer to haften to the affiftance of your unhappy country. Save the nation, the King, and your own head.

September the 19th, 1771.

The Sentence of Count ENEVOLD BRANDT, *at full length.*

IT appears, from Count Brandt's own confeffion, as well as from the declaration of the late prime minifter, John Frederick Struenfee, and from other circumftances, that Count Enevold Brandt was not only Struenfee's very good friend, but even his intimate, whom he intrufted with his greateft fecrets.

Therefore, in confideration of the royal favour and intimacy which he enjoyed, it would have been his duty to endeavour, by all means, to remove thofe things, of which he, according to his own declaration in his trial, difapproved in the conduct, fentiments, and tranfactions of Struenfee, and which he muft have found foolifh, audacious, and detrimental both to the King, the adminiftration, and the whole empire.

Inftead of this, he, as a criminal fubject and fervant of the King, unworthy of his truft, has acted in concert with Struenfee, and has not left off to be his intimate, and to affift him.

He fuffered himfelf to be employed by Struenfee to keep every body from fpeaking to the King, left his Majefty fhould be informed of what was blameable in Struenfee's conduct, in which he himfelf was fo deeply concerned.

He

He has behaved, not only in private, but even publicly, to the great concern of his fellow subjects, infolently, and without any refpect towards his King.

He has not fhewn that reverence to his Majefty which every good fubject thinks his duty, and expreffes readily from his heart on all occafions, in his words and actions: he rather has oppofed the King, that he might gain and keep Struenfee's favour, to obtain an extravagant fortune, and ferve his own private intereft.

His memoir, which is a kind of correfpondence between him and Struenfee, is a proof of his abfurd pretenfions, and that he acknowledged his blameable behaviour towards the King. Therefore he fhould have altered and amended his conduct, and rather have quitted a poft that he held, which he difliked, and for which he was not qualified. But no! he would not act contrary to the will of his benefactor and protector Struenfee, who wanted him, for his own purpofes, to be about the King's perfon; and Count Brandt, on his part, expected to be rewarded by his friend with greater honours and riches.

He in his department as *directeur des fpectacles*, has affifted Struenfee, to bring about a mifunderftanding in the royal family, by affigning to Prince Frederick a feparate box in the play-

houfe

houfe, left his Royal Highnefs fhould have an opportunity, by being in the fame box with the King, to acquaint him with Count Brandt's and his intimate friend's moft blameable conduct.

He has prevailed upon Struenfee to make him, within a fhort time, prefents out of the King's treafury to the amount of 60,000 rix-dollars, though he was convinced, he neither for his fervices nor for his conduct deferved fuch a reward.

When he returned his thanks to his Majefty for thefe great prefents, he did not mention the fum, becaufe he was confcious that he was un-deferving of it, and becaufe Struenfee had defired him not to mention it, left the King fhould get an infight into that, which the approved of extracts of accounts have fince clearly fhewn to his Majefty and every one who infpects them.

All thefe criminal actions are perpetrated by Count Brandt, and his confcience muft alfo tell him every moment, that he acted as a faith-lefs fubject, and particularly againft his duty and obligations on account of the efpecial favour and confidence his Majefty honoured him with: and befides all this, he was fo earneftly and fo fenfibly put in mind of his duty in two

anonymous

anonymous ·letters, which were found in his pocket-book, and wherein he was advifed concerning what he ought to have done, if he wifhed to preferve his head from the fcaffold.

He was ruled and guided by nothing but infolence, ambition and avarice.

Criminal as all thefe mentioned things are yet they are nothing in comparifon to what Count Enevold Brandt himfelf has confeffed, clearly and plainly before the King's commiffion, and what is proved and confirmed by feveral witneffes; *That he has laid hands on the facred perfon of his Majefty.* For it may be confidered, as if he had attempted to kill his Majefty, becaufe it cannot be foretold what the iffue of fuch an affault might be, and an unlucky blow on a tender part has frequently been the caufe of death.

He was angry at the King, and wanted fatisfaction of his royal mafter, whofe well deferved admonition he fhould have received with repentance of his former behaviour towards him, and fhould have avoided coming into his prefence, left he fhould offend him again.

Inftead of this, he planned with ·his friend Struenfee, how and when he could beft affault his Majefty, and confidered by himfelf, what weapons he was to ufe, which he kept in readi-

X   nefs,

nefs, though upon second confideration he did not make ufe of them.

Being told by Struenfee that the King was by himfelf, and that it was now time to put his defign into execution, he confiderately and with full intention to revenge himfelf, went to the King, turned the two pages that were in waiting out of the room, bolted the door, left any body fhould come in to oppofe him and to prevent his defign, and forced his Majefty by words and by an affault to make refiftance.

He wounded the King in this fcuffle on the neck, and abufed his benefactor and his King with words and expreffions fo fhocking and rebellious, that every body muft forbear repeating them.

Though Count Brandt has faid in his defence, that his Majefty had forgiven him this; yet, fuppofe it were fo, it cannot be underflood otherwife, than that his Majefty would forbear punifhing fo great a crime for a while. This indulgence does not juftify him, and his Majefty muft know beft how far it fhould extend itfelf.

This deteftable and traiterous action of Count Brandt, cannot be confidered otherwife than as an open attempt upon the King's perfon, and cannot fall under any other denomination than

that

that of high-treafon, which deferves the punifhment fixed upon fuch a crime in the Danifh
code of laws, book vi. chap. 4. article 1.

We, therefore, judging accordingly, think it
to be juft and right, that

Count Enevold Brandt fhall have forfeited
his honour, his life, and his eftates; that he
fhall be degraded from his dignity as Count,
and all other dignities which have been conferred upon him. His coat of arms which he had
as Count, fhall be broken by the executioner
on the fcaffold; likewife fhall Count Enevold
Brandt's right hand and afterwards his head be
cut off when alive, his body fhall be quartered
and laid upon the wheel, and his head and his
hand fhall be ftuck upon a pole.

Given by the King's commiffion at the caftle
of Chriftianfburg, *April* the 25th, 1772.

I. K. Juel Wind.　　G. A. Braem.　　H. Stampe.
　　(L. S.)　　　　　　(L. S.)　　　　　(L. S.)
Luxdorph.　　　A. G. Carftens.　　Kofod Ancher.
　　(L. S.)　　　　　(L. S.)　　　　　(L. S.)
I. E. E. Schmidt.　F. C. Sevel.　　O. Guldberg.
　　(L. S.)　　　　　(L. S.)　　　　　(L. S.)

The approbation of the King is as follows.

We

We hereby approve in all points of the fentence, pronounced by the commiffion of enquiry which we had appointed at our caftle of Chriftianfburg, againft Enevold Brandt, on account of his deteftable and traiterous defign and affault upon our own perfon, that he fhall have forfeited his honour, life, and eftate, fhall be deprived of his dignity as Count, and all other dignities which have been conferred upon him, his coat of arms fhall be broken by the executioner on the fcaffold; that his right hand, and afterwards his head, fhall be cut off when alive; his body fhall be quartered and laid upon the wheel, and his head and his hand fhall be ftuck upon a pole. Whereupon thofe whom it concerns are commanded to act accordingly.

Given at our caftle of Chriftianfburg, the 27th of *April,* 1772.

CHRISTIAN.

O. Tott

Luxdorph. A. Schumacher.
Dons. Hoyer.

F I N I S.